To avoid a prison sentence and subsequent criminal record, Janice Hutchings agrees to undertake an educational diversion plan, initially suggested by her mother, a renowned psychologist.

The program is supervised by Officer Manning, the arresting officer. She is a large, intimidating woman who, along with the presiding magistrate, firmly believes that the plan should also include suitable punishment.

Administered at the home of a brilliant psychologist and former student of her mother's, Gordon McGuire — a passionate penal reformist — the program is based on his revolutionary, intense methods. The lack of security, however, in his private residence means that permanent restraints are deemed necessary by both the officer and magistrate.

And so begins Janice's strange, eccentric journey, where her restrictive confinement and psychological experiments lead to the revelation of dark family secrets, repressed traumas and emotional upheaval.

The Diversion of Janice Hutchings
Copyright © 2024 Stephen Mottram
ISBN: 978-1-4874-4226-2
Cover art by Martine Jardin

Published by eXtasy Books Inc

Look for us online at:
www.eXtasybooks.com

THE DIVERSION OF JANICE HUTCHINGS

BY

STEPHEN MOTTRAM

EPIGRAPH

Passion without consent is violence.
Violence with consent is passion.

PREFACE

In 1996 a diversion program was introduced into the state of Victoria.

A diversion program is a method of dealing with a criminal matter outside of the court system that gives the offender a chance to avoid a criminal record.

If a magistrate agrees that you're eligible for diversion, you'll be put on a diversion plan. Certain conditions must be followed in this time, which may include undertaking a course of education.

If you follow the conditions of your diversion plan, the police drop the charges, and there will be no finding of guilt. This means no criminal record.

To be eligible for such a program, you must agree that you were responsible for the offence.

PROLOGUE

Silent, so silent,
Mustn't let the bogeyman hear me.
Dark, so dark,
Mustn't let the bogeyman see me.
Still, so still,
Mustn't let the bogeyman sense me.
Quiet, so quiet,
Has the bogeyman gone away?

CHAPTER ONE: CRIME

Janice

As I lie there with my eyes open, looking at the ceiling, my head moves in sync with Rob's rhythmic thrusts. My brain, however, resides in another place.

As I've never been one for sex, my energies are better served elsewhere. Like making money, which my profession as an insurance agent seriously facilitates. My latest project is a client I'd picked up from diligently calling some of my national company's dormant clients. That is, still on the books but no longer with an agent and having not done business with us for at least five years.

Actually, it was his wife I'd spoken to. Her husband had recently passed, and she'd told me she was thinking of calling my people right then. How opportune.

"Thinking of calling?" I should bloody-well think so. Her husband's life policy was worth two million dollars — money she's agreed that I should invest on her behalf.

My business thoughts are interrupted by restrained grunts as Rob's thrusts feverishly quicken. Instantly, instinctively, I concentrate on my beautiful husband as his warm, bodily fluid explodes from within and invades my body. I love it when this happens. When his passionate, utter desire is aimed entirely at me, continuing to thrill in a way I could never have imagined. Hardly, not with my bland, unemotional upbringing.

With a gentle kiss on my cheek, he leans over, whispering

in my ear, "Thank you, darling. If only I could do the same for you."

And that's when the guilt hits me.

I know how much his desire for me inspires him. A desire, unfortunately, I'm incapable of reciprocating, and I'm often left wondering what the devil is wrong with me. Unable not only to respond in kind, but to feel, *identify,* sexually. As a teenager, I mimicked my friends, lying there in bed thinking about all things supposedly passionate as I played with myself, but with no result. In the end, I dismissed it, concluding all will come to pass when I fall in love.

And I do truly love Rob—fuck, we've been together for ten years now—his tall, athletic frame as he walks off to the bathroom generating all sorts of admiration. But not in a sexual way. My turn-ons, if you like, are more the results of my hard-earned success. The refurbished Californian bungalow Rob and I own in Camberwell. The stylish car I drive, along with my tailored dresses, suits, and business blouses—a successful appearance in my industry is paramount.

But it's more than just my appearance. I genuinely enjoy the feel of my expertly fitted garments and their relationship with my body, which is tactile to the extreme. My perfectly arranged, buttoned-up garb provides both security and elegance while fitting in perfectly with my so-called *neat complex* as Rob describes it. Plus, it's compatible with my habitual nature. I do everything in a routine manner. Visit the same cafes and shops when I'm at the head office, travel the same route to get there, and park in the same parking lot. You name it, I do it ever so habitually. Yet another reason why my itinerant occupation is so good for me. taking me to all parts of the city, hurtling me from my otherwise routine existence, be it ever so stylish and opulent.

As Rob had been urgently in need of his latest executive stress relief, I discard both my panties *and* dress and toss them into the laundry basket for our housekeeper, Cathy, to take care of. A task she completes three days a week, along with the cleaning and food shopping. Then I turn on the shower and wait a few seconds until I've adjusted it to my taste before hopping in and luxuriating under its warmth, looking forward to tomorrow's appointment with my latest client. Thirty-five thousand dollars commission, who would believe? And all from a cold call.

My eyes close as the stream of hot water bounces off my face — could life be any better than this?

The next morning, Rob and I bundle into my car. Since it's a Tuesday, it's my regular weekly visit to the head office, and with Rob's car being repaired overnight and his mechanic's garage on the way, he's joining me.

With Rob sitting in the passenger seat, where I would normally place my banana, I hand it to him.

"And what do you want me to do with this?" he asks.

"It's my breakfast. Just hold it for now. I'll eat it once I'm on the main road."

"You and your bloody habits," he says, though good-spiritedly, before applying his seatbelt.

About a kilometre down the road, I put out my hand for my breakfast before checking myself. "Seeing as you're there, you can peel it for me."

"Yes, mistress. Anything else I can do for you?" he asks.

"Yes. You can toss the skin out the window when you're done."

"I'm not doing that. It's littering," he says.

"No, it's not, it's biodegradable."

Passing me the banana, which I start to eat, enjoying its unique flavour, he stares at me as if in disbelief. "Are you for real? Little miss goody-two-shoes breaking the law? I can't believe it."

"I don't consider it breaking the law. Eventually, it'll disappear."

"Well, I'm the solicitor here, and I'm telling you it's littering."

I glance across to see if he's being funny — clearly, he's not.

"I do it every morning," I say as I finish off the banana. Then I lean across and snatch the peel from him before winding my window down and tossing it out.

"What the fuck." Again, he stares at me in wonder. "I can't believe you just did that."

"You keep telling me I've got a neat complex, so no way it's sitting in my car."

He's about to reply when suddenly we're interrupted by the sound of a siren and flashing lights behind us.

"Told you." He chuckles.

"Jesus. I do the same thing every day," I say as I pull over.

"Don't worry. It's only a minor offence. Let me handle it."

"What? Don't be ridiculous. I'll tell him I'm sorry, give him my damsel-in-distress look, and we'll be on our way."

"So-called modern women. Don't mind falling back on old times when you need them, do you?"

But before I can respond in an appropriate manner, he turns, looking back over his shoulder. A huge smile appears on his face. "Though you can forget about that tactic. *He* in fact, is a *she*."

Looking into my side mirror, I see a stern-looking female officer approaching.

With my window already open, I smile as she leans over, addressing me. "Driver's licence, please, madam."

"Can I ask what this is about, officer?" I say as I rummage through my bag, Rob with a grin as wide as Port Phillip Bay on his dial.

"Your littering of the highway, madam."

"But it was only a banana skin, and that's biodegradable."

I pass her my licence.

"Still littering . . ." With Rob chuckling in the background she hesitates, reading my licence. "Ms Janice Hutchings."

Putting my licence in her shirt pocket, she then stands back. "Could you step out of the vehicle, please?"

Could I what?

But before I can respond, Rob intervenes. "May I ask what this is about, officer? Littering's only a minor offence."

Bending over, she peers through the window. "And who might you be?"

"Robert Hutchings, her husband."

"Good. You can drive her car when I take her to the station for processing."

Take me to the what? This is getting serious.

Again, Rob intervenes, this time forcefully. "You can't charge my client for a single littering offence. What's your number, officer? I'll be reporting your over-the-top behaviour."

"You're welcome to my number, but I doubt you'll bother when you see what I have on my dash cam. Your client, as you call her, has been committing the same offence for the last five days that we know of, possibly even longer. So, as such, I'm completely entitled to charge her and take her in."

We gawk at each other. Rob's face, and no doubt mine, appear in wonder at this news.

"Now, madam, as I said previously, would you kindly step out of the vehicle?"

Heart beating like billy-oh, I comply.

"Now face the vehicle and put your hands on your head."

My heart is now absolutely thumping. I barely notice as Rob, too, gets out of the car, a look of utter concern on his face as we stare at each other across the roof with my hands on my head as instructed.

As for me? I'm not sure what I'm feeling. Terror? Disbelief?

All I know is that the adrenalin is rushing through me as never before when she takes my left hand down behind me and cuffs my wrist—tightly, as though I'm some sort of desperado. With my right hand following, soon both hands are fixed behind me, rendering me helpless. Christ, I've never been so nervous, so, so . . . and that's when I realise what's happening. I'm not in terror, nor in the slightest way frightened.

I'm bloody-well excited.

And then, something that's never happened before—to me, at least. A tingling warmth in my *nether regions,* as my cold-as-ice mother once described them on the one occasion the area came into her focus. *Fuck me.* I glance desperately across, hoping to Christ Rob hasn't noticed my carnal response. My legal problem at that very moment is the furthest thing from my mind. Thank God. Clearly, he's seen my desperation, but not the reason behind it.

"Don't you worry, darling, I'll get you out of this."

Get me out of this? I'm not sure that's what I want. What the fuck? *Of course that's what you want, Janice. You can't sell insurance with a criminal record.* Speaking of which, I immediately think of my upcoming client.

"Rob, this morning's client. Can you ring Graham, my sales manager, and get him to handle it for me," I say. "Don't tell him what's going on. Just tell him I've got COVID, and he'll handle it. That way, I get my full commission."

Grasping my tailored arm, the officer guides me toward her car. I speak quickly before she locks me away. "Tell him half managed, half-capital guaranteed. He'll understand."

Hesitating, he seems absolutely flummoxed. "Client . . . client? What client? Who the blazes are they?"

With the officer's hand on top of my head about to place me in the back seat, I more or less yell my instruction. "It's all in my diary in my bag. Call Graham first, *then* come to the station to look after me."

The seatbelt is then buckled around my restrained body by my grim captor, and we speed off.

Grim captor. Restrained body. The words bounce around in my brain as I sit back and relax. Now, where was I? And all at once, my tingling warmth returns.

CHAPTER TWO: PUNISHMENT

Janice

Buttoned up in my tailored finery, I sit on the bench in the lobby of the police station, looking every inch a solicitor. Except for the fact that my hands remain cuffed behind. My arresting officer is at the front desk arranging some sort of accommodation for me.

However, I'm no longer in a euphoric state, or whatever the fuck it was. My mind snapped back into gear upon entering the station with people looking at me as though I was a criminal. Not to mention some low-life type, hands similarly cuffed behind, smiling at me from the bench on the other side of the room.

Jesus! Time to get serious, Janice.

Regretting the fact I had prioritised my client with Rob ahead of myself, I now wish he was here. The officer comes across, taking my arm and leading me toward a thick, reinforced glass-paned door which is opened from the other side by a tall, older male officer.

"The cells are chock-a-block," he says. "Put her in interview room two. It can't be locked, so keep her in her cuffs for now."

Her cuffs? They're not my fucking cuffs, mate. Hurry up, Rob, for Christ's sake.

Keeping hold of my arm, the butch bitch takes me to said room, opening the door before, surprising me no end, taking my cuffs off.

Rubbing my wrists, I stare at her. "Did you have to do them so tight?"

"Out there I did. In here, not so much. Come and sit at the table. I can attach you there, make you more comfortable."

Attach me? Am I some sort of object all of a sudden? A package being stored away for safekeeping? This being told what to do, where to go, where to sit, stand or whatever, is starting to get to me. Then, as my complete and utter lack of liberty hits home, I burst into tears.

Coming across, she takes my arm, forcing me to the chair. "Fuck me, you're only in the station. Wait until you're in jail."

Jail? Never have I felt so alone, so defeated. Even more so as she matter-of-factly attaches me to the table, hands cuffed in front, before leaving the room.

I can't, for the life of me, stop crying. This might be run-of-the-mill for her, however, it's anything but for someone like me. Bleak, colourless walls emphasise the room's loveless state. Its emptiness invades every fibre of my being. I'm not meant to be in a place like this. And it's then that I think of Mother. Not with any great emotion — as if. But even cold, unemotional Mother is better than here. Even grounding me for weeks on end. Oh, how I long for that strictness again, where at least there was some sort of love involved, however twisted.

The door opens, and in walks Rob. Dear god, the sight of his beloved face, the warmth of his arms as he comforts me.

"Oh, Rob, Rob, get me out of here," I say, crying even louder. "I'll do whatever it takes, anything. Just get me out."

Pulling back, he stares at me as though startled. "Darling, darling, of course I'll get you out of here. I had no idea you'd be so distraught."

Sobbing now, my hands fixed in front of me, I bow my head in resignation. "You were right. It was littering. And my mother was right all along. I'm so, so naughty."

Speak of the devil. The door bursts open, and in walks Mother — otherwise known as the redoubtable Jocelyn O'Donnell — in all her splendour, with the clearly angry arresting officer trailing behind.

"Get those cuffs off her this instant," she demands.

"Not so fast, Mrs O'Donnell. She has a serious charge to answer for."

"A serious charge? Littering? Are you joking, young lady?"

"Officer Manning, if you don't mind," she says. "And no, I'm not joking. Your daughter's been caught on my dash cam for the last five days at nearly the same spot, same time, throwing debris from her car window onto a busy thoroughfare."

Mother turns to me, staring that stare and taking me back to my childhood in an instant before thankfully directing her glare back to Officer Manning. So that's the bitch's name. Let's see how her bullying ways stack up against Mother Dearest. It's good to have her back, if only for her warlike ways.

What the fuck? Did I really just think that? Could this day get any madder?

"On your dash cam?" Mother says. "What in heaven's name were you doing, recording her for five days?"

"The first day I saw her doing it, I was booking someone else, so I couldn't respond. Then, the very next day, she drives past and repeats the offence. As I said, damn near in the same spot, same time."

Bugger my habitual ways. I knew someday they would come back to bite me on the arse. Tell you what, though, it's stopped my sobbing. Watching these two heavyweights slug it out, I decide the place is not in the slightest bit empty or lifeless anymore.

The bully bitch continues. "So rather than book her on the spot, I tailed and recorded her for the following five days, finally pulling her over."

Giving her a wry look accompanied by a grunt — I suppose

you could call it—Mother responds, this time though more cautiously, seemingly aware of her opponent's ability, not to mention courage. I'd never seen anyone stand up to my mother before, and this young lady is more than holding her own.

Mother is about to respond when the tall male officer who'd originally admitted me enters the room. "A quick word, Officer Manning," he says.

He whispers some asides to her and she smiles, nodding her head in gratitude, it would seem, before turning back to Mother as he leaves the room.

"It seems your daughter's minor offence has just increased exponentially, Mrs O'Donnell," she says. "Recognising her habitual ways, I thought it prudent to investigate our camera's recordings on that stretch of the highway at around the same time of the morning. And lo and behold, Ms Hutchings has been doing this since eighteen months ago, at the very least."

"Eighteen months? He couldn't have possibly gone through that much data in such a short time," Mother says.

"No. But after a few minutes of investigating the last month or so, he prudently jumped back to then. And there she was, as plain as the pretty nose on her face, blatantly scarring the countryside with her trash."

Fuck me. Putting my head down, I can still sense Mother's glare, however. Fortunately, she has other fish to fry. Although, this slippery eel of a police officer is far from the frypan.

"So what is it you intend to do with my daughter, Officer Manning?"

"I intend to charge her with littering with intent and in a recidivist manner."

"So it would go to court?" Mother asks.

"Indeed."

"And if convicted?"

"*If* Mrs O'Donnell? I should hardly think there's a defence here. Unless, of course, your daughter is clinically insane."

They both turn to me. *Clinically insane? Fuck that.* I'd rather go to jail than an asylum. Then I recall the fucked state I was in when confronted with just that prospect and reach into my skirt for my balls — if that's not too much of a contradiction.

"Is there another solution?" I ask. "I mean, I'm not really a criminal, and a record would end my career."

Officer Manning responds, "Well, as a matter of fact, you *are* a criminal, Ms Hutchings, albeit a non-violent one. And that's where your solution may lie."

"Go on," I say, for the first time in my life, jumping in before my mother, who looks at me in surprise.

"It's called a diversion program."

"What's that?" Mother beats me to the punch.

"It's a way of dealing with a criminal matter outside of the court system, giving the offender a chance to avoid a criminal record."

"I'll take it!" I exclaim.

"Yes, well, it's not as easy as all that, Ms Hutchings."

"For Christ sake, can you call me Janice?"

"Of course."

"And you?"

"Officer Manning."

Everyone in the room except her seems astounded by this response. However, despite the fact that you could cut the air with a knife, I carry on, anxious to hear her info. "So you were saying, *it's not that easy,* as I recall."

"Indeed. Firstly, a magistrate must agree that you're suitable — no, *eligible* for diversion. And given your circumstances, I would think so. In fact, I'll recommend it."

"So what does it entail?" I ask.

Mother is surprisingly quiet.

"You have to follow certain conditions, usually some sort of education," Officer Manning says.

"And what would that be in my case?"

"Littering, on a serial basis?" She pauses. "Probably picking up litter from the side of the road on which you offended."

"You mean, in an orange jump suit?"

"Something like that."

"And for how long?"

"I'd imagine you'd need to continue with your job weekdays, so probably for a year or two on the weekends."

"A year or two? What jail time would I get?"

"Jail time?" She seems astounded. "First offence, non-violent? I would say thirty days, reduced probably to ten with good behaviour. But surely, you're not contemplating that?"

"Ten days compared to two years? Perhaps I should," I say. "But no, I'm not contemplating that, Officer. My job's my life, the best occupation in the world."

I pause, thinking. The pair of them, and Rob — Christ, I forgot he was there — viewing me intently.

"What if I did a full thirty days imprisonment?" I ask. "Not in jail, but under strict supervision that would satisfy the magistrate that I've been suitably punished rather than just educated?"

Officer Manning appears sceptical, and Mother's seemingly astounded.

Regardless, I venture on. "What if I signed an agreement? That if I was, in any way, non-compliant during the thirty days, my diversion program would be scrapped. Then, I would instantly go to jail, landing myself a criminal record. Would that satisfy the magistrate?"

"First of all, it's not the magistrate you have to satisfy, but me," Officer manning says. "His judgement is based entirely on my recommendations. Secondly, there are no such facilities available, so it would have to occur in a private residence and be supervised by a suitably qualified person."

"Such as?" I ask.

"An officer of the law like myself."

"Would *you* do it?"

Now *she's* astonished. *I'm clutching at straws here, everybody, help me out.*

As if to fill the void created by Officer Manning's amazement, Mother jumps in. "What about an ex-prison guard? A guard from a female prison?"

Officer Manning turns to her, clearly still astonished, no doubt wondering what sort of a family she's jumped into bed with. Come to think of it, Rob seems of the same mind, his mouth agape as the officer responds.

"Do you know of one?" she says.

"I do, as a matter of fact. He's a former patient of mine."

"Patient?"

"I'm a psychologist."

"A *psychologist*?" Clearly, she's dubious, wary — to say the least. "What's this person like? What's their standing in the community? And what was their problem?"

"I'm not at liberty to reveal that. But he has an impeccable prison record, and more importantly, has become a leading light in his field of psychology."

"So what are you saying, Mother?" I ask. "That he would agree to such an assignment?"

"Agree? He would jump at the chance," she says. "A penal reformist, he's been toying with this idea of a voluntary, more intense and targeted approach that would both lessen the offender's term and more greatly rehabilitate them."

Officer Manning appears grave. "I would have to meet the man, satisfy myself that he's not some sort of whacko."

"He's hardly that," Mother says. "Indeed, once one of my better students, distinctions galore on his assignments."

"Hmm. Well, that's for me to decide, Mrs O'Donnell. As my prisoner, Janice's welfare and rehabilitation are of my greatest concern. A matter I take very seriously." She pauses. "That said, I do want her to pay for her crime in a meaningful way, so she'll never repeat her offence. Arrange a meeting at once! Provided he's everything you say, and he's agreeable and has the facility to enable this venture, then I *may* assent."

"Done," Mother says. "And as for my daughter, is she free to leave?"

Officer Manning walks across, talking as she unshackles me. "She is. However, there will be a surety of some kind of forfeiture, such as her passport. I don't want her running off to some foreign country."

Some foreign fucking country? For littering? This woman is clinically insane, and I'm in her clutches. Rubbing my wrists, I go to Mother — not Rob — forgetting myself and embracing her, her kindly pats on my back typical of her guarded response.

She turns to Rob. "Rob, I want Janice to come home with me for the present moment. Apart from all this, I have another matter of great importance that I wish to speak to her about."

Rob comes across. "Is that okay with you, darling?"

Surprisingly, I don't hesitate. "I'll be fine. Did you arrange for Graham to meet with my client?"

"I did, and he'll place the funds as you directed. Oh, and he hopes you get better."

"Better? From what?" I ask.

"Your Covid."

Laughing, we embrace then kiss each other tenderly before I turn and leave with Mother.

And that's where the matter lies. All being well, and me heading off to who knows where under the guardianship of an enthusiastic penal reformer — a former client of my mother, no less — while volunteering to be held under maximum security. Thoughts wander, quickly dismissed, the previous stirring of my sexuality banished, an aberration never to recall.

I've a need to return to my previous *normality*, no matter how unfeeling, no matter how asexual. And, of course, there's the tiny matter of my mother needing to speak to me on *a matter of great importance*. Now that should be beyond interesting.

CHAPTER THREE: SECRETS DISCLOSED

Jocelyn

Driving home with my daughter, I sense a strange melancholy lingering between us. Glancing across at her as she does at me, our gazes meet, and she emits the smallest of smiles.

Hmm, nervous. I can understand that.

I've no problem with observing her in this detached, professional manner, despite the fact she's my daughter. Truth be known, I've been treating her as such ever since the *incident* that took her father from us—speaking of which. "The matter I want to speak to you about? It concerns your father."

"My father? We've never spoken about him. I only have the barest idea of who he is . . . haven't even seen a photograph of him."

"Yes, well, there's a reason for that. An important one, the cause behind all of this."

"This?"

"Us. Our relationship."

"Is that what you'd call it?"

I glance across again, but this time she's staring, as if observing *me*.

Hmm. Eyes back on the road, my expression becomes grave.

"There's a reason behind my treatment of you."

"*Treatment*? I'm your daughter, Mother, not a patient."

"Oh, but that's where you're wrong, so very, very wrong."

"What do you mean?" she asks. "Am I some sort of psycho?"

"You know how I despise that term. But no, of course you're not. However, you may well have been, if not for my diligence."

Staring across at me again, her expression is wry. "*Diligence?* I could think of a better word for it."

"Oh, yes? And what would that be?"

"Repression, Mother, repression," she says. "You wouldn't let me do anything. Kept me cloistered from the world. Is it any wonder I have such a buttoned-up soul?"

"Buttoned-up?"

She looks down at her tailored clothes. "Not this, though that's part of it. No, I mean inside, especially sexually."

"Go on."

"Rob and I. He loves me so dearly, especially in the bedroom. But I'm incapable of responding. I *feel* nothing."

"Nothing?"

"Not during the act. Only at the end when he comes inside me. I love that, his physical expression of his desire for me. A physical desire, unfortunately, I don't have."

"That's interesting—"

"No, Mother," she says, interrupting me. "It's not *interesting*. It's shit."

I don't respond—just drive along allowing her time to settle down, to regain her composure. The reason I chose to confront her—no, *our*—problem in the car. There's nowhere for her to retreat, her normal modus operandi since puberty.

A few minutes pass, and I continue, "The prison guard, my former student. Your soon-to-be guardian."

Appearing unemotional, she stares straight ahead, saying nothing, while shuffling in her seat.

"He's a very intriguing person. Quite the genius, actually. I was thinking of introducing him to you regardless. But this event is affording me the opportunity. Funny how things work out at times."

"I never viewed you as a fatalist, Mother."

"And I'm not. It's our experiences, along with our nature, that make us who we are. For example, you throwing your rubbish from your car day after day. How long was it?"

"Oh, I'm not sure," she says. "A few years. Ever since I read that *Fit For Life* book. That's when I started eating a banana for breakfast."

"That long. Further emphasises my point. You were begging to be caught."

"Begging to be caught?" she says. "I didn't even consider it littering. It's a banana peel, biodegradable."

"That's what you told yourself to rationalise your behaviour. Why didn't you just leave it in the car and put it in the rubbish later?"

She appears shocked. "Do you have any idea the neat freak you've created here, Mother? I would no sooner have it in my car than slit my wrists."

"Again, a superficial reason," I say. "You could've used a small car trash bag."

"God, they're even worse."

"That's not the point. The situation was manageable, but you chose the easy way out. Why?"

"I just told you, I didn't consider it as litter," she says. "But go on, Mother, I'm sure your scientifically trained mind will come up with the *true* reason."

"You *want* to be punished."

"What? Don't be ridiculous. Do you think I'm some sort of latent masochist? Let me tell you, that's so far off the mark. I hate pain, despise it."

"Pain is not the only form of punishment, darling," I say. "However, that's beside the point. Perhaps I should put it another way. For some reason, something no doubt hidden deep inside, you believe you *deserve* to be punished. You're right, it's not that you want it, but more you feel you deserve it."

"Deserve it? Like I've been naughty?"

"*Exactly*," I say. "And there's good reason for me to believe that such is the case, something you'll understand soon enough when I disclose my secret."

We pull up at the lights of a main intersection, giving us both time to digest our words before looking each other squarely in the eye, something we haven't done for years.

Her brow furrowed, she looks concerned, or perhaps worse — scared, terrified. "What is it you have to tell me, Mother? Are you saying it's something I've kept hidden for years?"

"We're two minutes from home," I say. "Let's wait until we're there, and all will be revealed, I promise. The reason for your behaviour . . . the littering, your repressed sexuality. And indeed, for mine, especially the way I reared you."

The lights turn green, and we move a few hundred metres before turning left into my street, a charming, leafed cul-de-sac.

"God, does this bring back some memories," she says.

"Perhaps, young lady, perhaps."

I Purposely don't use my key and ring the bell, and we're greeted at the door by Mary, my maid of some twenty years, who gushes at the sight of my daughter — my reason for ringing the bell.

"Miss Janice, how lovely to see you. It's been too long."

Accepting her embrace in a reserved manner, more befitting of my good self, Janice replies, "And it may well be never again, after I hear what Mother has to say."

Viewing her askance, though with a grin, Mary chuckles. "I'm sure it's not as bad as all that. Your mother's bark is much worse than her bite."

"Not sure, she's never actually bitten me."

"Nor never laid a finger on you by my recall. Now let's get you both inside, and I'll bring a lovely hot pot of tea, then leave you to your business. It's shopping day today."

"Thank you, Mary," I say. "We'll be in my study."

"Right, you are, madam. I'll only be a jiffy."

With Mary off and gone, Janice and I enter my study and sit in the two large lounge chairs, a small coffee table between us.

"*Leather,* Mother," she says, as she sits elegantly in the chair. "I haven't felt that for ages."

"No, not in that vegan world of yours."

Observing my daughter as she sits opposite, she truly has developed into a delightful creature, a wonderful specimen of the modern, urbane woman.

"So? This secret?" she asks.

"Wait until Mary's left for her shopping," I say. "That will give us a few hours of solitude. In the meantime, I want to talk about my student, your guardian."

"You keep referring to him as though he's about to become my jailer or the like."

"Well, effectively, he is," I say. "You don't think that bulldog of a policewoman will settle for thirty days of tea and crumpets and some friendly psychoanalysis?"

"Heavens no. She'd have me in irons in some sort of dungeon."

"Oh, I doubt he'll go that far," I say.

"*That* far? What do you mean?"

"You heard what Officer Manning said. She wants you to *pay for your crime in a meaningful way so you'll never do it again.* And then there's your offer of *thirty days imprisonment, not in jail but under strict supervision* to show you've been *suitably punished rather than just educated.* All this so you can get it over and done within thirty days rather than collect rubbish on the highway for a year or two."

"Fuck no," she says. "I don't want to do that."

"Such profanity, darling. Never mind. The salient point is that what you want, a shorter, more targeted penalty, is precisely what he's preaching. Something that can be agreed upon in advance between the parties concerned while also agreeable to the authorities. In this case, you, him, and Officer Manning."

"Yes, well, I did say all that, and I prefer that," she says. "So why would he be suitable?"

"He'll keep you under restraint with strict supervision. And not only that, because you're effectively his guinea pig for his thesis, he'll interrogate you, which will be of great benefit to you both."

"*Restrain? Interrogate?*" She squirms in her seat. "Are you sure I can trust him?"

"Absolutely."

Just then Mary brings in the tea with a few biscuits, laying the tray on the coffee table.

"I'll be off now, madam, Janice," she says. "All the best if I don't see you before you leave, pet."

"Janice is staying a few days, Mary," I say. "So take your time. I'd like a few hours alone with her. We have something important to discuss."

"Lovely. Right then, I'll be off," she says. "See you in a few hours."

Pouring the tea as Mary leaves, I turn to my daughter, lifting my eyebrow. "Still the same, black with no sugar?"

"Please," she says, as she takes a biscuit from the tray, inspecting it. "These are vegan."

"Yes, dear, all prepared for your stay over. I even have gluten-free bread."

"That's dietary, not vegan, Mother. Multi-grain is fine." Taking a nibble of her biscuit, she sits back in her chair, then looks me in the eye. "Now ... this deep, dark secret of yours."

Pausing to contemplate, I've rehearsed this moment so many times over in my mind, knowing exactly how I would handle it, vitally aware of its importance in the overall scheme of things. "When you were young, five or six, one afternoon after school, your father tied you in a chair and used sensory deprivation on you so you couldn't see, hear or talk before locking you in a room."

I expect all types of reaction, but she barely moves a muscle. "Did he? I don't remember that."

"You don't?"

"Not at all." Lifting her cup in both hands she sips her tea, before gazing at me curiously. "I don't know what you expect me to say, Mother, or indeed what I should do. But I honestly can't remember a thing. Consequently, your news hasn't affected me in the slightest. You, however, appear greatly struck." Suddenly she starts, her eyes exploring mine. "What are you saying? Was there more to it? Sexuality?"

"Oh God no," I say. "Your father was the most asexual man on the planet."

Clearly relieved, she chuckles. "Runs in the family."

"No," I say. "That's where you're wrong, Janice. That type of thing is more behavioural than instinctive. Unlike your animal friends, we're mainly creatures of learning. Heavens, we even have to learn to walk, observing those around us. Our brains are so large we're born prematurely compared to all other species. Even apes, monkeys, the next most intellectual beings on our planet can cling to their mother as she climbs the trees more or less immediately after birth. No, I'm sure— like your memory of your father's dastardly act—your sexuality has been repressed. And most likely by me."

"By you? How?"

"It's clear now, especially in light of your lack of reaction to my revelation, that I completely overreacted upon coming home and discovering you in the room like that. That's why your father left, why I booted him out never to be seen again."

"So that's what happened," she says. "But that wouldn't repress me sexually."

"No, it wouldn't, not directly. But because of it, I vowed it would not affect you in any way . . . but especially sexually," I say. "That's why I hid you away, sent you to all-girls schools. I was paranoid, worried sick. Especially so later on when I discovered first-hand how such events on a young mind can transform into sexual perversion in later life, as I'm about to describe to you. The patient concerned, coming into my life about the time you reached puberty."

She's looking at me intently now, as indeed, no doubt I'm looking at her. Should be — I've never been so intense. I'm trying to alert my daughter here and to make her aware of what may befall her, which, to me, is of vital importance.

"A male client of mine . . . his mother and father, who was a hairdresser, tied him in a chair one day to cut his hair. He was about the same age as you were when your incident occurred, and just like you, he couldn't remember a thing about it. Being told by his mother late in life when she was suffering from dementia that *you were always a naughty boy . . .* so and so, name to remain anonymous . . . *your father and I had to tie you in a chair one day to cut your hair.*" I pause, reflecting on this case that had changed my life more than I could ever know. "I can still clearly remember what he immediately said upon her revelation. *Well, that explains a hell of a lot.*"

"In what way?" she asks, mouth agape.

"As soon as he tied up a girl, he got an instant erection — without fail."

"God almighty," she says, hesitating before chuckling. "That must have made him very popular."

"It did. But because he'd repressed the reason behind his

oddity as he called it, he had a terrible time throughout both his adolescence and manhood, wondering why he wasn't *normal*, whatever that means, and blaming himself. My point being, that as creatures who learn from our experiences rather than sense our way through life, incidents like these can have a marked effect on us as adults. Just as I feel this incident has had on you, even though you, like him, can't remember a thing about it."

"Well, Mother, I can see your concern, and I must say I'm quite moved by it. It's nice to see you so involved, so emotional. Because *that*'s what I missed the most in my childhood. Not my father, but a loving, caring mother."

Then, without the slightest warning, she bursts into tears.

Dear God, what to do? And before I know it, I, too, am sobbing like a baby, moving across and taking my child into my arms. The two of us standing and gripping the other ever so tightly . . . making up for long years lost?

"That's why I was so strict on you," I say. "I didn't want you to suffer any further untoward experience. Though the way you calmly responded, I think it was more my treatment of you that may have caused any problems with your sexuality, not that incident."

"Don't be so sure of that," she says.

Wiping my tears from my eyes with my handkerchief, I separate from her before looking her square in the eye. "What do you mean?"

Taking a tissue from the table, she wipes her eyes as we resume our seats, once more viewing ourselves from afar.

"When that police officer cuffed my hands behind me? I felt a tingling warmth in my *nether regions*, as you so discreetly once described them."

We laugh.

"Heavens, I was such a klutz," I say. "But back to your sexual reaction. Could this be related to your incident? What were your feelings? What was it that aroused you?"

"This is unbelievable, Mother. One day we can't say boo to each other, now we're talking like . . . I don't know, old school friends?"

"I'm sorry," I say. "Have I gone too far?"

"No, no," she says. "I love it. I'll tell you all, *and* without being charged three hundred dollars an hour."

Again, we laugh, seemingly happy in each other's company.

"It was the helplessness of the situation," she says, resuming. "How vulnerable I was, especially when being taken to a place without my will in her car. But — and here's the rub — as soon as I left the security of her back seat and was placed like a criminal in the police station, it instantly changed."

"That's a good sign . . . that you're associating it with love."

"Love? Officer Manning? Hardly."

"But you did trust her," I say. "You felt safe, secure, unlike at the police station."

"True."

"I'll have to disclose this to my associate before he takes you under his wing," I say. "He'll want to know all about it. Plus, he can reassure you that he won't take advantage of the situation."

"Are you sure he won't?" she asks, eyeing me curiously.

"Oh yes. I've never seen a more dedicated person. Other than his study, he won't have the slightest interest in you at all."

CHAPTER FOUR: INTRODUCTIONS ALL ROUND

Officer Manning

The door opens, and a bespectacled man with a full head of ruffled, dark hair and a beard greets me, a welcoming smile on his face.

"Officer Manning, I take it?" he says. "Please, come in, come in."

He takes me through to his lounge from the entry hallway, a neat, clean house of the Edwardian variety fills my eye. It's no more or less than what I expected of a home in this better middle-class neighbourhood, though, its tidiness is a surprise. Clearly, he's a man of means, this bastard—now to check his sanity.

"This scheme of yours?" I ask. "Gordon, isn't it?"

"Yes, Gordon McGuire. Take a seat, make yourself comfortable," he says. "Tea? Coffee?"

"I'd prefer to get straight into it if you wouldn't mind, Mr McGuire."

"Please, Gordon," he says. "And you? How should I address you?"

"Officer Manning," I say. "So, what's it all about?"

His somewhat startled expression soon becomes one of enthusiastic zeal as he leans forward in the chair beside me, adjusting his black-framed glasses as they slip down his nose, peering at his hands that move in rhythm to his words. "I

really think I can change the Victorian penal system benefi-
cially, Officer Manning. And in no small way."

"Yes, well, let's stick to the diversion program for the moment, shall we?" I ask. "The Janice Hutchings case in particular. I have a magistrate of similar mind all set to authorise
your little program if it serves our purpose."

He looks up at me. "You say of *similar mind*. May I ask what
that means?"

"You most certainly can, indeed. Once I explain all, we'll
see if your psychological nonsense is about to be blown out of
the water." He attempts to respond but I'm having none of it,
eager to get to the gist of the matter. "Magistrate Thomas and
I are of a similar belief that this diversion program is being
used to give people of Ms Hutchings's standing an easy time."
I pause, staring at him forcefully. "Well, we're having none of
it! They're to be punished, Mr McGuire, punished! So what
do you make of that? How does that fit into your cerebral
mumbo-jumbo?"

The look on his face . . . clearly, the silly bastard is in disbelief, as I knew he would be. As I'm about to rise and go, his
face at once begins to shine, setting me right back on my am-
ple arse.

"I can't believe my luck," he says. "It's exactly what I pro-
pose. A concentrated program of intense re-education, combined with maximum security."

Well, fuck me dead. "Go on," I blabber, more or less in shock.

"Yes, well, the strategy I have devised for Ms Hutchings is
designed specifically for the diversion program," he says.
"Where non-violent, though confessed criminals are to be
kept in private homes for their full sentence. No time off for
good behaviour, thirty days the minimum sentence involved
for it to have maximum effect."

I shut the fuck up, his enthusiastic gibberish music to my
ears. *Please, dear God, do not let him be a nutcase.*

"Now, I take it, as the prisoner's keeper, it's my duty to ensure she doesn't escape, such an event resulting in not only a loss of income for the current job but a future disqualification from receiving any further work?"

"That would be the case, yes," I say, responding to, rather than confirming, his proposal.

"That's very important," he says, his enthusiasm not in the slightest waning. "Not only for my motivation, but as an explanation to the inmate regarding the severe restraint she's about to receive. Shows it's not personal or done with zeal but merely business. The dehumanising of the procedure is a relief to them, putting their mind at ease."

Fucked if I know exactly what all that means, and while it seems good, I'm a bit worried about all this restraint business. "When you say restraint, Mr McGuire, what're we talking about here? Handcuffs, shackles, chains?"

He appears aggrieved. "Good heavens, no, Officer Manning. Such severity would defeat the purpose. No. I'm talking of the softest of ropes, applied with such diligence and care that while unable to move a muscle, the prisoner will be extremely comfortable. Here, let me show you. Put your mind at ease."

And with that, he presses a remote, and on the screen appears a woman, perhaps in her thirties, dressed in business clothes, a white jacket and black dress, trussed to a chair with a red ball gag in her mouth staring at the hand-held camera as it moves toward her. He pauses it, moving across and squatting down before the image, pointing at it.

"You see here? What I've done. The model has her hands behind over the back of the chair, and her body fastened to it at certain strategic points. And as you can see, she's perfectly happy."

"Who's the woman?" I ask.

"My neighbour from up the street. She has three children

and enjoys her time away from them . . . treats it as solitude."

"Solitude? How long is she kept like that? Clearly, she could never escape."

"Why thank you," he says, appearing chuffed. "It depends on her availability. But the maximum period of restraint is four hours, as it will be with Ms Hutchings."

"Four hours?" I ask. "And she can take it?"

"Loves it, finds it exciting," he says, before pressing the play button on his remote and returning his attention to the screen. "When we move to the back view, it shows how I have her absolutely fixed to the chair without applying any undue pressure on her arms. I have a younger model as well, in her mid-twenties. She's a psych student, second-year, and, like me, starting later in life. She does it to assist me and my particular thesis. And as she says, she *can use the money*."

Driving home from McGuire's, I'm as happy as all fuck — as I know Magistrate Thomas will also be. Hutchings is the perfect test case for McGuire's *treatment*, which he guarantees will rehabilitate his *patient*. Certain she'll never again litter while at the same time getting to the cause behind her misdemeanour, setting her on a remedial pathway.

I realise he's probably as mad as all fuck. But he's smart, articulate, and harmless — and an artist with those ropes. Fuck me, those girls were going nowhere. But most importantly, when I inform Magistrate Thomas of the breadth of her punishment, he'll be tickled pink. I'm already looking forward to McGuire's daily reports, where I'll get to see that smart-arse bitch get her comeuppance — middle-class, good-looking mean girls like her forever giving me buggery at school. *Who has the power now, bitches?*

Gordon

I feel on edge as I arrive at Mrs O'Donnell's home to collect her daughter for her thirty-day diversion program. Not about the actual program, I'm confident about that — its structure, its rules, its aims. No, it is the patient, or should I say inmate, Ms Hutchings, about whom I have misgivings. Her mother's information about her daughter's minor *brush* with her sexuality when handcuffed, is a potential fly in the ointment if ever there was one. The last thing I need is a besotted inmate, her judgement clouded by inflamed emotions ruining my proposed interrogations. This is its first trial, if you will, and I want it to be a true test of her intellect, not some kinky romp. Still, it's best to wait and see what happens. *Gordon McGuire, your clever brain can turn a positive into a negative as you usually do.* The myriad of twists and turns and capabilities of the human mind enable all sorts of possibilities.

The door opens, and I'm greeted by a middle-aged woman, who I presume to be her maid or the like.

"Gordon McGuire to collect Ms Hutchings for her diversion program," I say.

"Of course, come through. They're all waiting for you in the parlour."

Parlour? Have I stepped through some magical looking glass into the nineteenth century? And *all?* I would hardly call two people *all.*

And that's my first surprise. Beside them stands a tall, handsome young man in his thirties, I would imagine, about ten years my junior.

Mrs O'Donnell opens proceedings, walking across in her tailored splendour — as indeed is her daughter — her hand extended, which I shake.

"Mr McGuire, good to see you," she says. "This is Robert Hutchings, Janice's husband, and of course, while never having actually met, you know of my daughter, Janice."

I shake both their hands, noticing in particular my future inmate's demeanour, which fortunately seems calm and measured. Good. What with her husband here, all sorts of emotions could ensue—still may.

"Ms Hutchings's husband, Mrs O'Donnell?" I ask. "What on earth would have prompted such a move?"

Stepping forward, chin set, the aforesaid husband gazes at me squarely. "I insisted on making sure you know she's loved and that she's to be well taken care of."

"Well taken care of?" I ask. "What manner of a program do you think I'm running here? This is not some amateur hour. The entire procedure was run past and approved by Officer Manning and signed off under a magisterial order. The warrant for Ms Hutchings is in my briefcase, along with her restraints."

"My restraints?" Ms Hutchings says. "Am I to be bound for my journey in front of my mother and husband?"

"Yes to the former, bound and sensory deprived so that your location will forever remain a secret to you *and* your loved ones." I pointedly address Mr Hutchings with my final words. This scenario is exactly the type of complication I feared as soon as I'd laid eyes on him—heroic bloody grandstanding, so cliché.

"But no to the latter, Ms Hutchings. You're to be spared that embarrassment and the emotions it may evoke. And with that, may I ask that you, Mrs O'Donnell, and your son-in-law leave us alone. I have to inform my inmate of the rules and procedures she faces, ensuring she's fully aware of both her restrictions and indeed her responsibilities to her carefully tailored program."

Surprisingly, especially so with respect to her husband, neither party appears concerned—indeed gushing forth with their cooperation.

"Certainly," Mr Hutchings says. "My main purpose for being here was to load her luggage into your vehicle. I hope you have plenty of room." He chuckles, turning my eye to the six or seven suitcases in the corner of the room.

"Good God." I turn to the prim and proper young lady. "What on earth were you thinking, Ms Hutchings? It's only thirty days."

"Officer Manning said you wanted me to wear my normal weekday clothes to make me feel at ease," she says. "And this is what I wear for a working week, five different outfits befitting my profession."

"You'll only need two, three at the most," I say. "I have a maid who comes three times a week. She'll be given the task of cleaning and preparing your clothes. Worry not. You'll be at your splendid best throughout your confinement."

"Take the three on the left, Rob," she says before turning and embracing him tightly, he responds in kind.

"Goodbye, my love," he says. "See you soon. Hopefully cured and a more rounded person."

More rounded person? What a curious thing to say.

Ms Hutchings then embraces her mother. "Thank you for organising this, Mother. I love you dearly."

Surprisingly — and I say that taking into account the woman's normally stoic attitude — it's the mother who bursts into tears before immediately wiping them away with her handkerchief. "Good luck, my darling daughter. This may be the turning point in your life."

They then leave the room together, the husband collecting the three largest suitcases, leaving us alone.

"Now, Ms Hutchings, where to begin?"

"Firstly, by addressing me as Janice. This Ms Hutchings thing is all a bit formal, wouldn't you say?"

"No, inmate Hutchings, I would not at all agree," I say. "We're not going on a picnic together, madam. You're to be punished, and quite severely, I might add. So listen carefully to my instructions and obey them to the letter. Do you understand?"

"Okay, okay, there's no need to get upset, Gordon."

"There's every need for me to be *upset* as you so succinctly put it, inmate. For example, your lack of respect addressing me as Gordon. In future, you shall address me as sir and only speak when spoken to. Otherwise, ask for permission to speak. This is not meant to be a cakewalk, inmate, so if you want to stop or burst into tears, go ahead. Take your bags and run away."

Her look is cold, calculating — her mother's daughter. "I'm not the slightest bit afraid of what you have to offer, *sir*. Indeed, I'm rather looking forward to it."

"If you're referring to your previous, minor sexual response, your *moisture of joy* as I call it, I'm well aware of it and will be monitoring it accordingly."

This seems to take her aback, but only slightly. "So what now, sir? Is it your intention to bind me?"

"I'm sorry?" I ask. "Did you ask for permission to speak, inmate?"

"I did not, sir," she says. "I assumed we were in conversation."

"Conversation? Inmate, you and I will never be *in conversation*. Yours is to listen and respond."

"Isn't that what a conversation is, sir?"

Now *I'm* the one taken aback — and not slightly as was she. I'll have to take care with this young lady, who's not in the faintest way intimidated. Her obvious intellect is a challenge. I'm so looking forward to this.

"I want you to stand at ease, inmate, while I inform you of the rules and schedules that will be applied during your program. Do you know what that means?"

"I do, sir," she says as she takes the required position, hands behind, feet apart.

I circle her, assuming a position of authority as I instruct her. I have no need for notes. The rules and procedures ironed out with Officer Manning are firmly etched in my mind.

"The first rule is that if you, at any stage, right up to the thirtieth day, do not fully cooperate with my instructions, then all bets are off. They won't be forced since this is a voluntary procedure. But you will then be taken to a penitentiary to begin your full thirty-day sentence. This means that your future is entirely in my hands, inmate. That I'm now your God."

Do I detect the slightest of smiles, a barely noticeable upper curling of the lip? "Are you finding this amusing, inmate?"

"Slightly, sir," she says, her smile now undisguised. "I'm an atheist."

I stop in my tracks, and she stares straight ahead, her smile gone.

"Are you being impudent, inmate?"

"Not at all, sir," she says. "Merely responding as instructed . . . *not* in conversation."

Bugger me dead. Clever thing, using my rules and throwing them back in my face. *Passive disobedience,* as Ghandi would call it, putting the next thirty days into an even more promising light.

"Hmm. Good, well done," I say, recommencing my circumnavigation of her. "Now to the schedule. Clearly you can't be in full restraint twenty-four hours a day, no matter how cleverly those restraints may be applied. And trust me, they're applied most skilfully, your discomfort not an item."

"Thank you, sir," she says.

"Did I give you permission to speak, inmate?"

"Apologies, sir, I assumed you were seeking a response. I'll be more circumspect in future."

"Apology accepted. And you need to be cautious, inmate, for penalties will be prosecuted for any further indiscretions, starting from now. Am I perfectly clear?"

"Yes, sir!" She barks this out as if replying to a drill

sergeant in full disciplinary mode.

"Hmm," I say, a minor response, but enough for one as aware as she to recognise. Mustn't let her think I'm not onto her shenanigans. "Now, as to your schedule. There will be three four-hour sessions of maximum-security restraints. You need not be worried throughout these periods, inmate. At the worst, a slight tingle or numbness may appear in your arms, but I very much doubt it."

She says nothing, staring straight ahead.

"You have no comment, inmate?"

"Sorry, sir, I wasn't certain if you wanted a response," she says. "But no, it all seems perfectly clear. And, as you say, very safe."

"Yes, yes. That leaves twelve hours in the day. Three one-hour meal-bathroom breaks and one hour of swimming in the pool." I pause, standing still as I view her. "You can swim, I take it, inmate?"

"I can, sir, quite well."

"I'm enjoying your pithy replies, inmate," I say. "Do you know what pithy means?"

"I do, sir. Short but salient."

"Exactly," I say. "Well done. Short and to the point. Journalists often use it purely in the sense of its brevity, a disgrace. You'll find I'm quite the pedant, inmate."

"Permission to speak, sir?" she asks.

"Of course, I was expecting a response."

"You were, sir?" She starts ever so slightly, however, maintaining her stare straight ahead. "Are we in conversation?"

"What? No, not really, of course not," I say. "Though I thought it obvious a reply was more or less invited."

She stays silent.

"Wouldn't you say, inmate?"

"I was being circumspect, sir, as you so sagely advised, your term *more or less* leaving me in doubt."

Christ almighty, what have I created here? My very own Frankenstein monster? She's better at this than I am. "Quite so, indeed," I say. "But back to what we were talking about. The composition of your day. As for your sunlight, where possible, you'll be positioned outside once a week, which should be sufficient for a thirty-day period. I have a lovely garden."

"Permission to speak, sir?"

"Go ahead," I say.

"Thank you, sir."

"For what?"

"For your consideration and kindness, sir. It appears my confinement will be everything I hoped and more, leading to a successful conclusion for both parties concerned."

"If you're referring to your sexual response, even that has been allowed for. If, in fact, it becomes a problem. You may respond, inmate."

"A problem? In what way, sir?"

"That you become in need of sexual relief."

She remains silent. In response, I'm impatient with her. "Take it we're in a conversation, inmate," I say. "You have permission to respond accordingly, as you wish."

"This sexual relief you speak of? What makes you think I'll be in need of it?"

"You'll be unable to masturbate in your bed due to your nighttime restraints."

"I never masturbate," she says. "It does nothing for me."

"Remarkable," I say. "What does?"

"Nothing. That brief time with Officer Manning in her car was my first brush with it. It was quickly dashed once inside that horrible police station."

"Are you telling me you've never had an orgasm?" I say, my amazement unhidden.

Flinching at first, she does, however, keep her cool,

continuing to stare straight ahead. "No, sir, I haven't."

"Then all the more reason for concern," I say. "You well may become *ready to explode,* if you'll excuse the expression."

She chuckles, giggles, to be more precise. "I doubt that very much, sir."

"Be that as it may, I've made the arrangements. Every seventh day, this option of sexual relief is available if you so choose. Just inform me the day before or earlier if you're certain. It gives me time to prepare."

She remains silent; our conversation is clearly over with her seemingly deep in thought.

Walking across, I open my briefcase. "Time for your restraints, inmate. Hands behind as they now are, wrists crossed, if you will."

Chapter Five: Getting to Know You

Janice

Well, so much for his promise of being *comfortable*. It's true. His restraints, while stringent and forbidding, don't bite into my arms or put any undue strain on my body. Even when placed in my current position inside his van, lying snugly on my side on a mattress, wrists and ankles tied together behind and attached to the van's frame.

This will keep you secure for your journey. He spoke those words before depriving me of my senses and applying his restraints as though he were doing nothing more than securing a package. This objectification, unlike when in the police station, sends me even further into delirium — *this* is *my discomfort*.

From the moment he'd tied my wrists, I'd become his complete and utter slave. He could've done anything he wanted. And it was then I realised that this absolute dominance, fiercely amplified by the restriction of my bodily movements, was where I belong. Being told by him where and how to stand in Mother's house had served as mere foreplay to my present state, had my body dripping with his aforementioned *moisture of joy*. A term, which at the time, seemed ridiculous but now rings with the truth of the gospels. His offer of sexual relief is certain to be taken up. Indeed, if I could play with myself right now, I would. This constant flow from my vagina is driving me crazy. Fuck me, the irony of it all; my restraints, the very reason for my ecstasy, are keeping me from pleasing myself.

The one thing about having your hearing, speech, and sight taken from you is that it heightens your other senses. Not that this was noticeable for the first thirty minutes or whatever of my transportation, such was the state I was in. But after a while, although not exactly settling down, I've grown accustomed to my *companion.* Enabling me to ascertain that we're on a freeway far from the city — the flow of our journey smooth and uninterrupted.

Hmm, taking me to a country retreat? Sounds perfect. He's a strange one, my keeper. I think that's what I'll call him, better than guardian or jailer — they're so cliché.

And asking me what turns me on? I wonder what turns *him* on? Probably this stuff, though he swears blind it doesn't. *Me thinks he doth protest too much.* I might ask him about it on one of my meal breaks where I'm sure I'll have more freedom. Or perhaps I won't? Maybe he'll feed me? Oh fuck, why did I think of that? I'm gushing again.

Gordon

Reaching out of my van window, I press the code on the pad, and the large iron gate begins to swing inwards, allowing me to drive through. All the while, I'm viewing the rear vision mirror as it automatically closes. I don't know why I do that. It's clear it'll close, yet every time I look behind and check. That's just me and my careful nature, I guess.

Careful? I think it's a little bit more than that, mate. What was it you described yourself as to your inmate? A pedant, that's right — someone excessively concerned with formalism, accuracy, and precision.

Well, at least I got that right in my little spiel. Did I fuck that up? Trying to establish my authority and instead establishing hers. Fuck, she's going to be a challenge this one. A successful insurance agent is the toughest job on the block, where if you don't sell, you make bugger all. She probably knows more about communication and human nature than the whole of the psych department combined.

Looking over my shoulder, I think she seems perfectly content. Christ, even cosy as she lies there on the mattress secured to my van. She's certainly a fine specimen of a woman. Her immaculate tailoring highlights her athletic, curvy frame as she lies there. But unlike her, I don't view her bonds as an embellishment to her beauty. To me, they're just a means to an end. An opportunity to reshape Victoria's, maybe even Australia's penal code — all resting on the success of this venture.

Yet here I am, musing on her feminine charms. I bet she has feminine wiles, too. But so far, she hasn't presented them, seemingly content to serve out her time and escape a criminal record. But who knows? It may be nothing but a front, a ruse to make me relax, put me off my game — like a cobra, coiled up in the dark ready to pounce. Well, we'll see about that insurance lady. *I'm* in control here, *I'm* setting the agenda.

Speaking of which, how best should I handle her? Baffle her with science? That's what I'll do. For example, rules, explain them more fully. Oh, and your excellent binding technique. Go through it step by step as you're tying her. Jesus, I've spent years developing those. That's got to impress her. Yes, that's what I'll do. Pile on the detail, and she won't know what hit her. By the time I'm finished with her, she'll want to be left alone in her ropes, eager to relax as best she can and allowing the time to while away ever so slowly as she progresses her way to freedom.

Janice

Blah, blah, blah, blah, blah, blah, blah – who does he think he's kidding? Trying to make out he's not interested in me, just the process. Who gives a fuck why he has to tie me so tight to the chair? Obviously, he doesn't want me to escape. That's a given. But his enthusiasm? It's more than about his rope techniques, I can tell. A man doesn't have to have a fat in his pants to show he's excited. There are tell-tale signs, like he displayed in our first meeting and as he does now. Subtle things, like the dilation of the pupils in his eyes – Jesus, they're like moons in there. The same way a woman's nipples respond, as I've recently discovered. Christ, they've been erect for ages now, pressing against my expensive bra, suit jacket, and business shirt. I swear he'd only have to touch them, and they, and I, would probably explode. He did warn me of that, that I might become *ready to explode.* He got that right.

Clearly, there's something going on beneath his cold, indifferent exterior, and it's not just about how good he is at tying me. For instance, his adjustment of my jacket when the ropes pulled on its front, accidentally folding it, and how he carefully placed it back down, smoothing it out precisely. Now if he was only concerned about his ropes, he couldn't give a fuck about me, could he? Sure, fair enough, when he told me to *sit up straight, put your arms over the back of the chair* and *slide your bottom back so that it touches the back of the chair,* they're all to do with my positioning. But to correct the lie of my jacket? That's *all* about me.

He's behind me now, carrying on with his endless chatter. "You'll notice, inmate" – he's sticking with his formal approach, probably to distance himself, dehumanise me, *us* – "I've cleverly tied the loop that fixes the upper part of your thighs, up near your torso, under the bottom of your jacket front" — the part he fucked up, then corrected — "not only to the chair but also to the rope between your wrists, which I've left reasonably apart for your comfort, then attaching them to the chair, as well."

He's not expecting a reply, except perhaps a grunt of acknowledgement as he's already gagged me, placing a large, soft stress ball in my mouth. Squeezing it first before inserting it, he'd then allowed it to expand within my mouth, completely filling it but with no chance of me swallowing and choking. Clever that. He'd then wrapped a wide black stretchy medical bandage very, very tightly several times around my face, squeezing my cheeks ever so hard while carefully keeping my hair from within its grasp before gently adjusting my locks when he was done, once again sending signals. If it was just about securing me, as he so laboriously claimed prior to my *rigging,* as he calls it, then he wouldn't be worried about a lock of hair out of place here or there, would he? Of course not.

The silly bugger probably doesn't realise it himself. Wouldn't imagine he's had too many romantic experiences in his life, yet another thing I must raise on one of my *meal* breaks, along with the small matter of what turns *him* on. He can't stop me from talking when I'm eating, can he? Can't gag me then, even if my hands are tied and he's feeding me.

Fuck, there it goes again, a tiny spurt of my friend down below at the mere thought of such helplessness, dependence. Why in the fuck does something like that turn me on so much? I can't wait to get home and get Rob to try this out on me. I wouldn't be lying there thinking of commissions then. Instead, I'd blow his socks off. Fuck, I might even blow him, which is something I've never even thought of doing until now.

He comes back in front of me. Now what's he doing? Oh fuck, he's about to blindfold me with the same black material he used to gag me. Be still my flowing moisture.

"After I've blindfolded you, Ms Hutchings, I'll be applying some headphones with birdsong coming through. It's all you'll hear, but because of its pleasant sound, it should serve to relax you. I won't be applying this in all sessions. In some, such as when I'm interrogating you, I'll need you to be able to converse. But for your initial session, I thought it appropriate. An induction process, if you like, to help you get accustomed to your confinement, your loss of freedom." He pauses, looking at the time on his mobile. "Late afternoon. I assume you're not particularly hungry?"

I shake my head.

"Good. Once your four hours are up, I'll give you some supper, then prepare you for bed after you've attended to your toilet, cleaned your teeth, or whatever else you need to do. Is that clear?"

Nodding my head, I shut my eyes as he wraps the material around them several times, cutting out all light before applying my headphones, the relaxing birdsong sound coming through loud and clear at once. A gentle tap on my shoulder and he's gone, or at least I think he is. He could be sitting there watching me, observing me. Most likely not. It sounded like he was busy, eager to get things done. Instead, he's probably writing some notes about today and our first meeting.

That's the thing about being a prisoner I'm quickly discovering, especially in my excessive situation. I no longer have a say in what happens around me or how it affects me. All is entirely up to my keeper. Clothes—not in my case, thankfully—diet, though again, he's assured me my vegan diet and supplements such as B12 and iron will be maintained. And what I hear, see, and even what I talk about, if such a privilege is allowed.

But *not* my thoughts—those are entirely mine with the birdsong not interrupting them at all. Instead, it provides the perfect background for serious contemplation, which of course, being the analytical soul I am, I immediately set about doing.

Try not to think about him. He has no control in here. Rather think about, no, sense what's happening to you, both physically and mentally.

Now, let's see — physically. I'm more or less completely restrained with thin, white rope on a sturdy wooden chair with a padded seat. My upper legs are looped three times and cinched firmly to the chair seat. This means that the rest of my legs, from just above the knee down to my ankles, which have been tied and cinched separately by four further loops, come back to the chair at an angle. My ankles are then tied and cinched to the chair rung between its front legs, pulling my high-heeled feet back under me and then further tied back to my wrists, pulling them down.

Just like the hogtie he had me in, in the van, but sitting in a chair. It's as though he has purpose-built the chair specifically for me, which he probably did, though I could imagine him going to various stores, inspecting all sorts of wooden chairs, and puzzling all the store assistants with his complicated inspections. A smile comes to my imprisoned lips.

But back to my legs — trying to move them, I find they barely shift. The slightest movement sideways is my only relief. I'm fixed, going nowhere, as he said I would be. But as he also said, I'm entirely comfortable without a skerrick of pain — so he's not all talk, thank God.

As for the upper part of my body, having placed my arms over the back of the chair, he's firmly attached my upper arms and torso to the wide rail at its top by the most highly engineered arrangement of ropes one could ever imagine. Fuck me. He took a photo of it, *me*, from behind, then showed it to me. I'd already seen the front view as he'd placed a full-length mirror in front of me so I could *admire my handiwork* as he had weaved his magic.

Several loops of the thin white rope ran horizontally above and below my breasts and from over my shoulders behind my neck and back under the rail, pulling my torso down as well as holding it fast. However, the fascinating thing was that he'd also joined the two strands above and below my breasts with a smaller, vertical strand in their middle, which, when combined with the two vertical strands on either side that came from my shoulders, more or less encircled my breasts — highlighting them. At first, this intrigued me, thinking he was sexualising me, but he was so concentrated on his rigging that I'd quickly dismissed this as fanciful.

Regardless, this elaborate positioning meant that while my torso was firmly attached to the rail, so too were my upper arms, with my elbows below comfortably bound about ten centimetres apart. It was ingenious and intricate and the whole thing was finished off by pulling my wrists, which were bound about five centimetres apart, down toward my ankles, as well as being attached to the strand of rope that ran around my lower torso that he was going on about earlier.

His piece de resistance to his *masterpiece,* however, was the continual vertical strand of rope connecting my body, back and front. Beginning with the rope that ran across my shoulders behind my neck, he'd pulled it down tightly to my elbows, further pulling my shoulders back. My elbows, then, pulled down toward my wrists, and they, in turn, pulled down toward my ankles. Then, at my front, my breasts — ah, that was why he'd tied that rope there — tied to the first of the three loops that held me fast to the padded seat in front, before finally connecting it to the other two. This continual vertical strand he finished off by looping it horizontally with rope, giving it a pipelike, sturdy, immovable look — like a chain.

Whew, it tires me out just describing it — but not him. He was so passionate when rigging me, a process that took upwards of twenty minutes, which *quite fairly and due to time constraints, is to be deducted from your four-hour session.* Yet throughout, he'd maintained his passion, his pupils absolutely dilated at its end. Hmm, perhaps his work *is* the reason for that, not me. I'll have to think about that.

Certainly, he's made an impression on me. The fact that I could so accurately and in so much detail describe his ultimate showpiece is amazing, to say the least. But given I was literally a captive audience—I suppose I had little else to do but observe.

That said, it wasn't as though I was at all disinterested throughout his escapade. I truly was fascinated by his ingenuity, but even more importantly by my passionate urgings that rose in concert with each stage. Starting with my arms and upper body and culminating with my lower legs being attached to the rung of the chair, by which time I was, in fact, *ready to explode,* such was the violence of my discharge.

Which leads me to my other response to my situation—that of the mental variety. And that, in itself, is a story to tell. Christ, a saga. So where to begin? Perhaps it should be at the end, when, at the completion of his artistry, he'd shown me the photo he'd taken from behind. My wrists were bound five to six centimetres apart, attached both to my body at their front and pulled down firmly toward my fixed ankles, unable to move—at all. The utter captivity of my entire body was reflected, not by his elaborate design, or his piped rope work, or his creative engineering—but by these helpless hands. Fingers cupped, they hang passively as if in resignation, all avenues lost except those of acceptance.

And that's the person I've become. Passively, resignedly, accepting of my fate, but not in despair or with lack of hope. This complete dependence on another brings with it a state of both peace and enlightenment. And I'm able to see who, in essence, I truly am for the first time.

I want him to come back and talk to me because I feel we're kindred spirits, though clearly on the opposite side of the coin. Yet I don't want him to unbind me. My deliverance, if you will, brought about by a peace not stemming from freedom, where I was lost in some vast wilderness, but by the centring of my soul into a singularity. The *last* thing I need is space. Give me confinement every day where all that I am can be focused into a person *ready to explode.* He's right, I am. Like a giant star whose gravity finally overwhelms it, causing it to implode, but thereafter creating new life, such as our own solar system, or in my case — this version of me.

Christ, what's happened to me? I've never waxed so lyrical. But that's how I feel when I'm like this. Sure my body is alive with passion — fuck, yeah. But above all that, or perhaps alongside it, is this feeling of belonging, of purpose, and not in a singular, solitary way. For example, how I would love him to come back and fuck me right now. Of course he's not about to. I don't really want him to. It would ruin a great friendship — *LOL.*

The big question is, *why?* Why do I feel this way? But as Mother says, and she ought to know, we humans *learn* things. Very little, but the basics, are innate and instinctive. So where did I learn this from? Is it what my father did to me? But that's not a part of me. I didn't even know about it till Mother told me. But it wasn't part of her former patient either, the guy who cracked a fat as soon as he tied a lady up. As far as he was concerned, it was innate, only to find out later on that it was learnt, a moment forming just who he was, as my favourite singer-songwriter Sarah Blasko said in her emotional love song, *Here.*

But he hated his kink despite his success with the women — whereas I love mine. Though in the end, when he'd discovered the truth, a load was taken from his mind, relief that he wasn't some sort of psycho — sorry, Mother. But I'm the opposite. Lying under Rob feeling nothing made me feel more like a nutcase, not this. Who knows, who cares? All I know is that I'm in a dream, a dream I'll never leave.

Chapter Six: Release of a Different Kind

Janice

Day seven of my *diversion* program — how apt has that word become — I'm about to receive my sexual relief. I wonder what he'll do to me? All I know is that it'll involve machinery, not him, as he'd sternly told me after I'd raised the subject about *what turns him on* during one of my meal breaks — where no, he didn't feed me, bugger it.

Speaking of which, I'm even hornier than before. No wonder, being severely restrained under *maximum security* for four hours three times a day before being left as I now am in my bed. Spreadeagled in my nightie, held by four wide leather cuffs with the doona carefully placed over me by him, further arousing me as he'd bid me *goodnight, inmate*.

That's what I get now. No more *Ms Hutchings*. Christ, I reckon he'd be calling me by a number if he had more than one of me. This process of dehumanising me is certainly working, making me feel more or less completely objectified. However, it's a consequence that merely adds to my heightened state of arousal.

Impatient, I shift around as best I can, looking at the ceiling for the umpteenth time. I'd never slept on my back before, always on my side. It was a bit difficult at first, but I soon got used to it, as I did with my *ring* gag — an unforgiving instrument that forces my mouth wide open, allowing me to breathe through my mouth, as well as my nose. It was as though he was doing me some sort of favour.

What time is it? Christ, I hate not knowing, though it adds to my excitement. How fucked is that? All I know is that it's early morning, and the birds chirped their daybreak chorus only an hour or so ago. He'll be here soon, bursting through the door as cheerful as ever, enquiring after my health as if it might have changed in the eight hours since last he'd left me.

We have no discussions during my daily restraint periods as I'm always gagged, with the extent of my sensory deprivation increasing as the day progresses — a blindfold is added for the second period, and speakers with either birdsong or white noise complete my isolation for the third. However, during our meal breaks, we have normal conversations, chatting away like people do in workplaces everywhere, except for my hand and foot manacles. All of which disappear during my magical one-hour swimming sessions held in his indoor facility where his heated twenty-five-metre lap pool is located. I do so love the freedom of those one-hour sessions, relishing my ability to freestyle, backstroke or whatever I feel like doing. Though I'm not to frolic, this hour is to be used purely for exercise *keeping you healthy, supple.* Yet when I'm finished, I look forward to being restrained again in his masterful way. This midday hour before lunch is just enough to whet the appetite, refresh my mind — clever bugger.

And here he is.

"Good morning, inmate," he says as he opens the blinds, allowing the soft morning sunshine to come through. "I trust you had a good night's rest? Big day for you, your first orgasm, I suspect."

Orgasm? Incredibly, I hadn't even thought about that, focusing on the journey and not the destination. Isn't that the opposite of how people normally think? — which is hardly surprising in this topsy-turvy, upside-down world I've entered, my own version of Alice's Wonderland.

But now he's brought it to mind, I'm so up for it, especially so as he unstraps my cuffs, leaving me to unbuckle my gag. Thus, beginning this most eventful of days on my own steam, a purely temporary situation, no doubt.

"Have your shower and do your other bits and pieces, but don't bother to dress, inmate. Clothes aren't required today."

Normally, I'd have been shocked by such a command, but not anymore. Six days of severe restraint and isolation does that to a girl — wearing you down, turning you into a submissive soul despite the constant titillation. Oh, and a tactile one. Heavens, I had no idea how sensitive I am with my choice of outfit in the mornings becoming super important — more about how I *feel*, rather than how I look. A six-button, double-breasted suit with a pencil skirt, business shirt, pantyhose, and heels further extending the restraint on my body with the tight ropes squeezing their already-fitted formality against it. Whereas a satin blouse with a longer, softer, more feminine collar buttoned up to my neck creates a new sensation, with the tightness of his ropes virtually touching my skin as they alone imprison my body.

But no matter what circumstance I face, what surprise befalls me, throughout it all, my eroticism constantly burns with my moisture of joy commencing immediately when I stand before him, ready to be positioned. And today, wearing nothing but what Mother Nature has provided, these dual sensations burn even brighter, as my utter vulnerability tears at my brain. Dear God, the ropes soon to bite into my skin — fuck me, what will that feel like?

"We shall not be using the study for your release today, inmate," he announces, interrupting my thoughts, a slightly wicked smile on his face.

He's not going to put me outside, is he? Like he did the

afternoon of my third day, pulling my arms up behind me and attaching them to a branch of a tree – *strappado,* as he called it. Thoughts of me staked out on his lawn with all types of mechanical stimulation attached to my naked body instantly flash through my mind.

Knowing I'm not at liberty to speak, he continues. "No, today we'll be visiting the basement."

He pauses, overtly observing my reaction, which I manage to keep suppressed – externally, that is. However, my mind, heart, and pussy are responding gloriously, the thought of brick walls and chains with irons hanging from them transforming my enthusiasm into euphoria.

Coming over to me, the dilation of his pupils is as ever as he heads behind me, applying a collar around my delicate neck. This, however, is not your common, garden-variety collar – the three buckles rather than one tightened behind my neck are a testament to that. Lengthy, its hardy leather forces my neck into a strict, vertical position, keeping my chin up and instantly registering a change in our status.

This marked contrast between his relaxed, stress-free state compared to my enforced, strict deportment takes our relationship to a still greater level. This simple act of *collaring* turns me into his slave, and he into my master, even though he gently guides rather than forces me down the steps, holding my hand delicately as he leads the way. A prince leading his princess down a staircase as they make their entrance into a grand ballroom. Christ almighty, be still my beating heart. I don't know what he's got planned, but it won't take much. My first orgasm, I sense, is a mere heartbeat away.

Upon reaching the floor of his *dungeon,* as pictured in my mind, I soon see that it's anything but. The brick walls remain, but not a chain is in sight. In their stead, various steel contraptions stand, together with a round, wooden post with horizontal rails sticking out from its sides, which he leads me to.

"Hands behind, inmate. This post is to become your companion for the next few hours. Your body and it to become as one."

For heaven's sake — nothing should be as delightful as this. With my crossed wrists pulled behind and my arms over one of the horizontal rails, I feel the softness of the material he's using as he fixes my wrists to the post. Looking across at a table through my sexual haze — since that's what I've become, a prisoner of my inflamed emotions — I view the various long, flat strips of material with only the slightest interest, my mind patently on other things.

Please, please hurry up!

With his ceremonial attitude sending me balmy, next he meticulously binds my legs above and below the knees to its lowest rail, stretching them apart. Then he slowly and surely ties my waist to the post at another rail, its thongs joined to my already affixed, crossed wrists. However, my elbows remain noticeably untied. There's no need because they're helplessly resting over a rail and going nowhere.

Then — is it the final piece of his puzzle? My neck is fixed with one of his soft strips so I must look straight ahead, with my posture collar further ensuring this goal. His entire, elaborate arrangement — as he had suggested it would — fixes me to the post.

Straining as best I can to see what's going on, I'm aware he moves a black steel stand with what appears to be a large vibrator held on an arm pointing upwards at an angle over to me, flexible at the joint between the arm and the stand. He moves it up and down slightly so that eventually, it pushes gently against my clit — the same organ that was as dead as a doornail when lying in my bed as a teenager, but now is as alive as all hell, causing me to flinch.

Oh Jesus, Jesus, Jesus, what's it going to be like when he switches it on?

With his deep brown dilated gaze looking straight into

mine and his face only inches away, he smiles. "What you feel touching you, inmate, is what's known as a *Hitachi* wand, the vibration of its large rubberised head able to be regulated at various speeds. I'll be starting you off at a low speed, the aim of which is to bring you to a slow climax, ensuring your first orgasm is a pleasant, calm experience."

By now, my mind and body are frantic, as his face disappears from view while he inspects me below.

"Normally, at this stage, a lubricant is applied to ensure there's no friction between the instrument and its recipient," he says. "But clearly, this isn't required in your case."

I would hardly fucking think so. It's been gushing down there for ages. For fuck's sake, man, send me on my way—all this ritualistic bullshit, it's sending me spare.

Coming back into view and with his face yet again quite close, his gaze looks into my helplessly affixed one as he smiles—this time though with a twist on his lips. "Before I switch you on, inmate, just one further condition, ensuring you're aware of your captive status even when in a euphoric state."

Further condition? What more can he do? Who gives a fuck? Anything, anything, just do it.

"You must ask permission before you cum. And regardless of your level of arousal, it may or may not be granted. Do you understand, inmate?"

Nodding my head as frantically as I can, considering its captive state, he smiles, switching the instrument on.

Oh. Fuck me. Fuck me, fuck me, fuck me. "Permission . . . to . . . come . . . sir?" I squeeze out, and a look of utter astonishment comes over his face.

"*Permission?*" Clearly flummoxed, he splutters his response. "Good Heavens . . . yes, yes, permission granted, permission gran—"

But before he can finish his words, I explode, screeching at first, then, groaning as all my repressed sexuality comes to the fore. My body contracts into involuntary spasms within its bonds as all the good reports I'd heard about such a moment come to fruition. *Jesus, Jesus, Jesus,* such a release of hormones or whatever the fuck it is. I continue to writhe and twist, and with my captive state playing havoc on my brain, once more, my body reacts. This time though less violently, but more intense as blurred visions of me in school uniform—what the fuck—flash in and out of my brain, intensifying my experience. But still, my torture continues—*no, no, surely not*—as yet again, my body stiffens before sending me into an absolute frenzy, and flashes of me in uniform, appearing anew as I cum.

Christ Almighty, I can't take any more of this.

But as quickly as it had come, it disappears—replaced by an unbelievable calm. With my muscles relaxing as they never have before, I slump, his straps and rails more or less holding me up against the post.

Immediately, urgently, he sets about untying me, his powerful arms catching my slumping body when he's done before carrying me over to a wooden bench.

Laying me down, he tenderly caresses my face. "Congratulations, dear inmate. Your first orgasm, and a triple, no less."

Coming out of my haze, I'm so confused. Flashes of me in uniform? What the fuck was that about? But that's not why I'm muddled. My bewildered state is more about the intense emotion I feel as he leans over, gently stroking my brow, my cheeks. His affection for me is as plain as the nose on his face. My own feelings are as I've never before experienced, with my desire to have him take me—in all senses of the word—overpowering. Christ, I've never felt like this with Rob. What's happening? Is my orgasmic experience colouring my judgement?

But all such thoughts are instantly demolished as, without warning, his strong, tender arms sweep me into his embrace.

His lips possess mine with all the fervour of a storybook hero. Capturing my no longer confused mind as feverishly I respond, all previously held inhibitions thrown to the wind. *This* is what love should be, unconditional outpourings of one's soul — passion released fearlessly, unrestrictedly, carefreely, if there's such a word. Who cares? Ours is the language of love — universal, multilingual. Never have I been so alive.

Feeling his ever-so-hard member enter me — fuck, that hardly hurt at all — I don't even bother to open my eyes as my arms automatically envelop his hard body, my legs wrapping around him in a loving but forceful embrace that drives him even deeper inside. I've become an animal, a beast. With my needs at this moment purely carnal, once again, I feel my sensations rising. However, this build-up is even greater than before, with the presence of my conqueror, my rescuer, my master, adding to my passion. And then it happens. The most joyous of feelings as, overflowing with emotion, I accept the warmth of his bodily fluid shot into me at an alarming rate. My own body responds in kind, arms and legs gripping him fiercely as — fuck, did I just bite him? I cum.

However, his response to my violence is anything but negative. Lifting me from the bench as I cling to him, he, in turn, bites me, thankfully in a loving way, on my neck. The sensation as he sucks my blood to the surface is un-fucking-believable.

Still inside me, he pushes me against the wall with the pair of us peering rather than staring at each other, clearly wondering what in the fuck to say. Me? I stay mum. Not completely aware of what had just happened, I wouldn't know what to say anyhow.

Eventually, he smiles. "Well, at least now you know what turns me on."

Unable to take my gaze from his, I smile. "And what's that?"

"Love, inmate, love."

Love? Did he really just say that? "Love?" I feebly enquire.

"Yes, love. Unlike your good self, who's infatuated by other, more worldly events such as her bodily entrapment."

"I think what we just experienced was about as unworldly as one could ever find," I say, my cheeky, alert self returning as I continue to cling to him, his shirt still on, pants nowhere to be seen.

"Ah, yes, but motivated by matters of the mind, body, and not the heart."

"Is that right, sir?" I ask. "Well, let me tell you what I experienced just now . . . I've never before experienced, *especially* with Rob. And I used to think I was in love with him."

"Used to?"

"Well, clearly I'm not, am I?" I ask. "Not after experiencing what love truly is."

"So are you telling me you love me, inmate?"

"I suppose I do."

"Suppose?"

"Let's get things clear here, *kind, sir*," I say. "I'm sure I don't have the first idea of what love is. But after today, I do know what it's not. What I had with Rob is of the latter variety. What we had, however, had me *flying to the moon,* as they say in the classics. So doubting that I'll ever find better, and regardless of what initially aroused me, namely my restraints, it was in your arms that I finally felt like a woman. So if that means you tie me first, my foreplay if you like, then, afterwards fuck me when I'm free, so be it. I'm more than happy with that."

"As am I," he says. "As long as you realise that tying you up is not sexual for me, and I never want it to be. Its intent for me is purely professional. You and you alone are my inspiration. Something I haven't experienced since losing my wife, Elizabeth."

Carrying me back to the bench, he sits as I stay astride of him while thankfully, he unbuckles my posture collar. With that moment passed, I'm eager to hear his story.

"So, what happened, Gordon?" I ask. "Can I call you Gordon?"

"You can, as clearly our business for the day, your sexual release, has been obtained. But it's back to *sir* tonight when I strap you in."

"You don't want to sleep with me?" I ask.

"Oh, I do, very much. In fact, it's my intention to do so on a daily basis once all this is behind us."

"Daily?"

"I don't do things in a half-baked fashion, Janice."

Well, didn't he slip that in beautifully. And never has my name sounded so lyrical. "I was going to tell Rob it was over, regardless."

"You were?" he says.

"Yes. I've been thinking about having him bind me, but his heart wouldn't be in it. Plus, there was the other small thing about me falling head over heels for you basically from the moment I met you."

As he's smiling gleefully, his eyebrows raise. "Hence your response."

"Hence my response," I say. "Now, your wife? You were about to say?"

"Elizabeth, yes. The only woman I ever said *I love you* to. And until today, I assumed the last, burying myself in my work instead." He pauses. "She died of cervical cancer just under ten years ago. Like you, she was very attractive, but more importantly, again like you, a caring, vibrant soul. Her death was the reason I visited your mother professionally, to help get me through it."

Again, he pauses, suddenly returning to his former businesslike self. "There's the matter of my daily reports to Officer

Manning, which remain vitally important if we're to get her to drop your charges and secure your release."

"Daily reports?" I ask. However, as interested as I am, I have no intention of releasing him from my grasp.

"Yes. The photos I take both at the start and end of your bondage. They're taken on her camera, the time and date are permanently imbedded by her beforehand to ensure their legitimacy. According to her email replies, she's extremely happy with your treatment."

We chuckle. "I bet she is. We must never let her know I actually enjoy it."

"*Enjoy*? That's one way of putting it," he says. "That's the reason why I tell you at the start of our sessions to look serious, not to smile. At the end, of course, with your pretty face enclosed, you're basically unrecognisable."

"So, I have a pretty face, sir?"

"Indeed, and a womanly figure, inmate, as no doubt you're aware," he says.

A thought springs to mind, dampening my triumph. "We didn't take any photos this morning. Won't she be concerned?"

"Not at all," he says. "I told her this morning of your request for sexual release, and she understands."

"Do you think she'll tell Rob?" I ask.

"Good heavens, no. Does she even know him?"

"Not really. We first laid eyes on her when she arrested me. And Mother did all the talking at the police station."

He smiles. "Yes, well, time for some lunch, then a stroll in the garden. You with your clothes back on and this time without restraints."

"*Without* restraints?" I ask. "We'll see about that, my darling, we'll see about that."

Chapter Seven: Unexpected Developments

Officer Manning

With my hands resting on the soft mattress behind me and my head back in a glorious pose, I sit astride of my lover, listening to his endearing words.

"Fuck you've got beautiful tits."

"Tell me more, my love. Tell me again how Rubenesque I am."

"Yes, yes. Your beautiful curves, your shapely behind —"

"*Shapely*?" Stopping, I lean forward, staring down at him.

"Shapely, yes. In a beautiful way, my love," he hurriedly says. "Your voluptuous arse is all that any man could ask for."

Rising from him, I'm not so much annoyed as disappointed as I sit on the side of the bed, my back toward him. "You've done it again, Rob. You know how sensitive I am about my behind. You've got to be more careful with your words."

But Rob has a way with his words that soon place me back on my cloud.

"Robby loves his beautiful lady, his imperious goddess. Please, dearest lady, come lay by my side and resume our sweet nothings."

How could a woman resist? Turning, I lie by his side facing him, and immediately, his creative hands explore my breasts as only he can, bringing them and me to life.

As I return the favour, gaze still fixed on his, my hand slips down to his amazingly hard penis, making me feel once again *the empress you truly should be*, as he so often tells me.

"I see your pee-pee is as hard as ever, my prince."

"As ever when in your majestic presence, my love."

"Tell me how beautiful I am again, Robby. Over and over and over until my body is so wet that it can't help but invite your glory inside."

"Fuck, that's a bit rich, even for you," he says as he rolls me over and enters me from behind, his favourite position.

Oh, Jesus, I never get sick of his rigidity inside me. And does he know how to use it. Fucked if I know what he saw in that scrawny bitch. Well, she is when compared to me. Not that she's on the scene; the thought of her strict security and Rob's constant bonking sends me into rapture as I cum for the first of what I'm sure will be many times this afternoon. Fortunately, though, Rob is much slower than I in his response, with his rigidity usually remaining long enough to allow my three orgasms to his one — the perfect lover.

Completely relaxed and lying there on our sides facing each other after our more than successful coupling, we start our usual after-sex chatter. Some people smoke, we chatter.

"So, tell me again, Officer Manning, why are we doing this to my wife?"

"Because she's an entitled, white, middle-class bitch," I say.

"All three of which you could be described as."

"Fuck you, Rob. There's nothing middle-class about me, unlike the skinny cunts that ruined my life, constantly telling me how fat I was."

"Yeah, yeah, I know all about that. Get over it, mate. You've grown into a magnificent specimen of womanhood with the best rack I've ever laid eyes on."

Leaning across, I kiss him gently on the lips, then, resume my position, gazing at his handsome face.

"But as I was saying, what's the main reason we set Janice up that morning?"

"Well, we didn't exactly set her up," I say. "She did litter, and she did do it for months on end."

"Yes, but because of me, you knew how habitual she is and that she didn't think she was littering. I mean, you could've pulled her over the first time and simply explained the law and sent her on her way."

"Don't make out it was all my doing," I say. "You were fucking-well sitting in the car with her, knowing what was about to come down."

"Yes. But thinking of her all tied up for thirty days, it's a bit rough on her."

"You can't blame me for that," I say. "When I brought up the diversion program at the station, I was expecting her to be picking up rubbish on the highway on the weekends for at least a year, hopefully, two, giving us time to be alone together to make sure we were truly in love. But then, when her mother came up with her solution, I had to respond. Otherwise, it may have looked suspicious. Besides, I thought the lunatic she's with would have been horrified when I informed him that she had to be punished, something, as it turns out, he's an expert in. Doesn't matter, it's giving us thirty consecutive days together, and after the first week, I'm now certain you're the one. As are you, I assume?"

"Christ, yeah, I can't get enough of you," he says. "Thinking about that frigid bitch just lying there . . . I shudder. What was I thinking?"

"You were both young. Certainly *she* was, leaving home as she did at eighteen to escape her domineering mother. Any wonder she fell for the first man that came along. No offence, darling."

"None taken," he says. "And she's a looker. So once again, I could be excused. Though if I'd known how completely sexless she was, I'd have never gone near her."

"Not to worry, everything's turned out in the end. We've got each other, and she'll remain an insurance agent." I pause. "The curious thing, however, is that he's informed me that she's taken up the program's offer of weekly sex relief."

"She *has*? I find that hard to believe. Probably just trying to get out of her restraint for the day. She's clever enough, trust me. Like the woman in the Iranian hostage crisis who took up smoking so she could get a break from being tied in a chair."

"Did she? I didn't know that." Again, I pause, thinking about how best to phrase my next words. "Janice must never know that we were an item prior to her arrest or indeed that we are now. Otherwise, she might suspect she was entrapped."

"So we *did* entrap her?"

"Clearly," I say. "But she was breaking the law, so she got her just deserts. Regardless, we've got to be careful how we handle this."

"Hmm," he says, reflecting. "How about we stage it so that you come to me — her husband *and* solicitor — after her diversion program is over to see how she's doing, unaware that she and I have split up. And that's when we fall in love."

"Sounds good," I say. "Yeah, that'll do. We'll set up an appointment in your office so your secretary knows and becomes a witness to our innocence. No one knows about us, do they?"

"Not on my side. You?"

"No bastard knows anything about my business at work," I say. "And you're the only man who's shown interest in me for ages."

"Ever since I saw those boobs of yours on that witness stand as you fearlessly stood up to my questioning, I've been enraptured. And then, when you came over to me after the trial? I couldn't believe my luck."

"You're a good-looking man, Rob."

He chuckles.

"What?" I enquire.

"You've got no idea, have you?"

"About what?"

"How sexually attractive you are? Even though you're a size sixteen or whatever you are, you're a tallish woman with a nice shape, your hips and boobs much larger than your waist. Plus, I absolutely love your *wobbly bits* as you call them."

Fuck me. I'm so overcome by his kind remarks, tears form in my eyes. *Jesus, stop it.* But when he comes over after noticing my emotional response and hugs me, it's all too much. Collapsing into his arms, I sob my head off.

"There, there, my love," he says.

I try desperately to stem the flow, embarrassed as all buggery about being such a weak bitch in front of him — in front of anyone. *I'm Officer Manning, the toughest cop on the block; fuck, even he doesn't know my first name.* Just shows I'm not as hard as I think. That I'm still susceptible to favourable comments from a man, the type of behaviour I deplore in other women. Weak, dumb bitches, that's what I used to think. Not anymore. My apologies, ladies, Rob's longing for me has a far deeper effect than I suspected.

We gently separate from each other, and I glance at him as I wipe my eyes with a tissue.

He gazes back, his hands softly touching me as he speaks. "It's nice to see the tenderness in you, darling, letting your guard down. The world isn't your enemy, you know. Nasty childhood experiences are where they belong — in the past."

In the past? I stare at him. Perhaps he's right. My treatment of his wife, amongst other things, is more or less a chance to get back at her type, rather than her personally. Yet I was quite happy to ruin her life, as I had previously done when faced with similar circumstances. *Huh.* Maybe he's also right that *the world isn't my enemy.* I never thought I viewed it like that, but he's spot on. I've been treating every bastard, especially Janice's type, with an equal measure of disgust and distrust.

With my mind cleared, I give him a quick hug. "Thanks, Rob," I say. "Clearly, I needed that. I think you might be good for me. At least I haven't ruined *her* life. She'll finish her program in a few weeks, and we can put it all behind us."

"Exactly. Get on with our lives," he says. "Perhaps even have some children together, something that would've appalled me with Janice. Further proof we were made for each other."

Children? I hate the little bastards—the less I see of my nieces and nephews, the better. But my estranged foster sister was the same way, and she's had five of them. Fuck, imagine that? No thanks.

I smile. "Perhaps, my love, perhaps."

Janice

As I lie here on my bed, the morning after admitting our love for each other, I've never felt as vulnerable. Not from my restraints or my open, spreadeagled position. No, this particular vulnerability stems from bonds of another sort—the bonds of love. Will he still love me in the morning? Was it just a momentary fling that will disappear as quickly as it came?

He was extremely affectionate as he put me away for the night. He placed my doona over me before adjusting my pillow to make sure I was extremely comfortable. Then he gently kissed me on the forehead—his tender lips sending my heart soaring yet again that day.

As it had after he'd bound me tightly for our walk in his

garden yesterday, my bonds due to what I would describe as my constant persuasion, rather than, as he had called it, my *nagging*.

I have to admit I was somewhat selfish in my attitude, forgetting completely that, unlike me, he wasn't enchanted by my bonds but purely by me — thus ruining our first tender moment of equality for him.

Although I'd quickly adjusted this stance at the end of the day when we'd had our evening meal together with me unfettered for the first time. It was so enjoyable, so peaceful, and so much fun talking about this and that and exploring each other in the kindest way possible. We were discovering little things about ourselves, like the type of wine or food we prefer, our favourite movies, and theatre, all the while exploring our individual sense of humour through our cheeky banter. Private intimacies that are every bit as precious as sexual ones, intimacies that I now find have left me feeling so very, very vulnerable.

I've read poems about this, describing *the bravery of love,* something I never truly understood. But now I do. True, we didn't need the same courage most lovers need when taking that first plunge — opening our hearts, risking rejection — with our exaggerated circumstances more or less ensuring we fell into each other's arms. But now, as I wait for my lover, wondering if today's moment will be the same as yesterday's, I tremble in my boots.

Fuck this thing called love. This is true vulnerability — emotional, tearing-at-the-heart stuff. It's entirely different and far less thrilling than any physical exposure, the submission of my heart rather than my body opening me up to the most torturous, the most terrifying pain imaginable as I lie here and wait for my fate that's entirely in the hands of another.

The door opens. My eyes close, my heart quivers as he walks beside me before going across and opening the curtains. Returning to my side, he sits on the bed.

"Good morning, dearest inmate," he says. "Ready for yet another exciting day in our valley of dreams?"

I've never heard such sweet sounds or viewed a more wonderful sight as I open my eyes to his smiling, clearly affected face. *Oh fuck.* He still loves me, he does, he does, he does — though he hasn't actually said those *three little words* as yet. Tender emotions sweep through my body, loving thoughts invade my mind, as he unbuckles my gag.

"Kiss me, darling, kiss me," I plead as soon as I can. But he doesn't. Instead, he's looking at me in wonderment.

"*Kiss* you, inmate?" He looks me up and down. "With you in such captivity?"

What the fuck?

"No, my love, such pleasures shall have to wait until our next sexual relief day, which I believe is seven days away. You, in the interim, are to be treated as any other prisoner should. With the utmost respect but also with the utmost caution, your captivity is paramount."

"Is that right? Seven days? I can't last that long," I say, pausing as I think how best to defend my case. "What about you? Do you intend to wait that long?"

He smiles in a smartarse, confident way. "I do, even if it means going to bed with boxing gloves on. What's good for the goose is indeed good for the gander."

"Gordon, you can't be serious," I say.

"Oh, I am, my love. One of us has to be, and clearly, to my utter delight, it's not you."

"Your *utter* delight?"

"Oh, yes," he says. "Wondering throughout the night whether your affection for me would continue."

I laugh out loud.

"What's that all about?" he enquires.

"Oh, my darling man," I say. "I've been lying here half the

night and all morning wondering the very same thing."

I swear he's about to lean in and kiss me, and ever so affectionately—but he does nothing of the kind, his disciplined and scientific mind coming to the fore.

"We have much to do in the next six days, inmate," he says. "Your punishment to ensue, your mind to explore."

Punishment to ensue, mind to explore. All at once, my body takes over, and the tingling warmth below is followed immediately by the gentlest of trickles. My anxiety is gone, and my passion has returned. And with it, the greatest of vehemence.

Gordon

My beautiful prisoner has dressed herself in a satin blouse with a long, slightly rounded collar at the top, buttoned up to her neck. Together with a tight pencil skirt that sits loosely around her waist, instead, her hourglass figure is so shapely that her hips are holding it up. Fuck me, what a creation.

I'll be going out of my way to observe such things for the rest of her program, with her every move and reaction to be studied minutely if I'm to get the most from my study. A task I now realise will require all of my powers of discipline, considering my deep affection for her. I never thought I'd ever feel this way again about another human being, but dare I say, my feelings for Janice seem even more intense. Perhaps it's merely our exceptional circumstances, perhaps not—time will tell.

"I think I shall place you in what's known as a *ball tie* for your morning session, inmate. But without your gag, since I have lots of questions for you, many avenues to explore." I pause. "I realise this freedom may put a strain on our professional relationship, but I believe it's better to face that problem sooner than later."

Standing there as she does with her hands behind her, waiting to be bound, my darling stares straight ahead, clearly playing her part to perfection. I decide to ease her way — oh, and mine.

"You may treat us as being in conversation, inmate, speak at will," I say, as I begin her rigging — starting with her elbows, not pulled together, comfortably apart, however, rendering her entirely helpless.

"I'll do my best, sir, to make it through the next week. But I fear I face a serious paradox. One of which I believe you should be fully aware."

"A paradox, inmate?" I ask. "That's a strong word. Perhaps you mean dilemma?"

She chuckles. "Back to your pedantic self, I see, sir. Let me explain, and then you can be the judge."

"Go ahead, inmate," I say, intrigued, to say the least, as, after tying her wrists — again comfortably apart — I truss her body. The tightness of the body ropes ensures the permanence of her captivity without compromising her comfort, which is a matter now of even greater concern.

"My problem is this. I still want you to tie me as tightly as you can, sir. The more helpless I am, the hornier I become. But at the same time, I want my mind to remain focused . . . detached so I can best answer your questions."

Stopping my binding, I come around and face her.

"The last thing I want, inmate, are confected responses. If you truly want to assist me in my study, firstly we need to put our affection for each other aside. Your concerns for me, as a consequence, are neither here nor there. And secondly, behave as you normally would, as you have up till now. I want you to become as horny as possible or whatever takes your fancy at that moment. This is the time to put your clever mind aside and relax and enjoy yourself, if that's what you want to do. Forget about me. Just because your bondage doesn't turn me on doesn't mean you should be the same."

"But, sir, won't you be offended?" she says. "Think of me as strange, crazy?"

"Good heavens, no, not in the slightest. Who knows why you react this way? But it's only with your completely natural response that discoveries such as these will be unearthed. So please, please, please, Janice, be true to yourself. I'll continue to love you no matter what."

"*Love* me?" She faces me and confronts me. "Say it, say those three little words. I dare you."

"*Dare* me? Never has a task been less daring, the words to flow" — I hesitate, searching for the right phrase — "like water over a fall."

She waits, her eyes beckoning, encouraging.

"Of course I love you. That's me, Janice Hutchings, all or nothing at all," I say. "I'm afraid you're stuck with me, for better or for worse, till death do us part — all that stuff."

The smile on her face, I could kiss her forever. But I don't, since she replies. "I'll be as perfectly natural as I can be wonderful, sir, revelling in the rapture of your sweet, unforgiving bonds. Take me to where my passions yearn, to a Shangri La of pure, unadulterated sexuality, so that my only escape is in the arms of your love."

"Fuck me, that's very good, inmate, very good," I say. "Ever think of writing a novel?"

"Never in my wildest dreams," she says. "My soul, sir, has been the driest, most dispassionate going around until I met you."

I chuckle before gently guiding her to the thickly carpeted floor of my study. "On your loveliest of behinds, inmate," I say. "Time to put you into a tight ball so that wriggling your fingers may be the only movement possible. Though I could also stop that if I've a mind."

The wondrous look on her face. "Could you? Oh please, do

your worst . . . or, in my case, best. Capture me, sir, so that not only escape but all movement is impossible."

"I shall, dear inmate," I say. "However, for the moment, I sorely need your beautiful mouth and ears for my research. But rest assured, all such liberty will eventually be taken from you come your evening session."

I'm behind her, blindfolding her, and is that a sigh I hear?

Chapter Eight: Lost in the Woods

Janice

"Rise and shine, inmate. We have a big day ahead of us."
He's awoken me, which he's been doing regularly for the last week. The sleep mask that he's given me has kept out all light, especially the early morning sunshine that used to creep through, causing me to wake early. Then, I realise it's my sexual release day. Thank heavens. The last six days, while exciting, interesting, and fulfilling, have served only to make me as horny as I imagine any woman has ever been. I couldn't envisage being more randy — the place for such poor souls is the asylum.

As clever hands take my mask off, I'm greeted by his handsome face. Well, it is to me, in a rugged, intellectual sort of way, if that's not a contradiction in terms. Anyhow, I know what I mean. He looks smart but not bookish — manly with his not-too-bushy beard.

Sitting on the bed, he takes off my ring gag while smiling. "Have a good night's sleep, my love?"

"Oh, I did, master." For the last six days, without prompting, I've been calling him that every time I'm bound before him — which is naturally most of the time. By now, we're in conversation at all times except when he tells me otherwise, which he does every now and then to spice things up or if he wants me in full prisoner mode for an *interrogation*, which is really a psychoanalysis session.

"I have a surprise for you today, prisoner."

Uh-oh, *prisoner*? What's this all about? I'm dying to ask him, but his subtle remark has forbidden any such intrusion as I remain silent, watching as he releases me from my spreadeagled placement.

"We're going on a picnic."

A picnic? Where? In his garden, I would imagine. His need for secrecy, as far as I'm concerned, is bordering on paranoia, if that's the right word. Probably not. It's more like obsessive or fanatical. Listen to me — are his pedantic ways beginning to influence me? More than likely, everything else about him has, as I would expect being his prisoner twenty-four-seven.

"Whereabouts? I hear you asking."

Exactly — hardly clairvoyant of you, my master.

"Believe it or not, we're going outside the grounds," he says. "And no, I haven't suddenly become rash, prisoner. Privacy where you're concerned is still paramount. No, my friend has a large estate, and he's informed me that, for the next few days, it's mine with no one there to disturb us. What say you to that, inmate?"

"I feel very privileged, master." I love playing these little role plays within our major role play, the Margot Robbie in me emerging.

Freed, I sit up and move my shoulders and arms about, luxuriating in their freedom and looking forward to my hot shower as I muse on what I should wear for my upcoming adventure. That's right. A picnic is now an adventure, and this tiny reflection brings with it a reminder of my captive, institutionalised state — further arousing my already inflamed libido.

But let's face it, I could think of flying to the moon or doing my tax return in my present condition and find that horny. Jesus, I'm so looking forward to my upcoming sexual release. I think I packed a summer dress away with my all-purpose, black, three-buttoned blazer, which should be perfect for our spring outing.

He's placed me in full sensory deprivation for our excursion, obviously to keep his friend's property's location secret from me. As he lays me on my side on the mattress, I'm hogtied and attached to the frame of his van — exactly as I was on my initial trip. This time, however, I'm not wearing a fitted suit and business shirt with pantyhose, but a flowing, full-length, floral cotton dress with no hose, my black blazer's three buttons undone — free as a bird. And, as it's my special day of the week, no bra and no knickers. I feel magnificent, wondering what he has in store for me.

The morning had passed with a light but lengthy breakfast conducted under inmate silence, followed by my swim pushed forward from its normal midday time. This prolonged silence is doing its job of creating sexual tension — if that was his aim.

With my hair dried and scented body back to its splendid best after my swim, I lie there gently discharging my amazing moisture, which has become, in its various strengths, my constant companion. I wonder what it'll be like when I'm back to my *normal* working self, whatever that will be. I'm sure I'll be able to control it when I'm with a client. Hope so. The slightest of trickles is certain to be only a fleeting memory away. God, that will take discipline. The starry-eyed office girls in love that I used to laugh at come to mind. Perhaps that's my fate. Certainly for a while after my release, I would imagine. Maybe forever — this entirely peculiar, life-changing event is so far removed from being traumatic, there's not a chance in Hades of it becoming repressed.

The van stops, and soon I feel his hands taking my restrictions from my face, and as much as I adore them, it's always a relief when this happens. Blinking at first, I look out through the opening of the sliding side door opposite at the

beautiful greenery that awaits me as he kneels beside me, untying my bonds.

"Off you go, inmate," he says at the completion of his task.
"There's a blanket laid out on the grass for you. Make yourself
comfortable."

Walking around the van to the blanket that's laid out on
grass rather than lawn, I see all types of trees surrounding it.
He must have noticed me taking in my surroundings as he
too comes from the van bearing a basket full of food and a
couple of bottles of water.

"Impressive forestry, isn't it?"

I stay quiet, well aware that he may be testing me, my prisoner status as yet not lifted.

"Very good, my love," he says. "You certainly have become institutionalised, haven't you? You may respond. Assume we're in conversation mode."

My freedom is such a relief, especially in such expansive
surroundings, prompting a need to fully express myself.

"Oh, Gordon," I say. "This experience is overwhelming
me."

Placing the foodstuffs from the basket onto the blanket, he
peers at me.

"Is that right?" he asks. "Amazing. Just two weeks of confinement, and here you are, overwhelmed by a picnic. This is
exactly the type of feedback I'm after, with my concentrated
penal experiment having the desired effect."

"It really has,'" I say. "Even though I absolutely adore my
captivity, it still has an effect on the psyche. Locked away, severely restrained, nearly always under some form of sensory
deprivation takes your mind into an entirely different place."

"Go on. I'm listening attentively," he says, placing the food
on open plates between us as I lie on my side, resting on my
elbow.

"Hmm, how best to explain it? Let me see. I love being

under your care, having you in complete control of me. For instance, you only have to say we're in prisoner mode right now, and you could bind me as you see fit." I look him square in the eye, softly, perhaps mischievously. "Now that's daunting in its own way. And I'm in love with you."

"Your meaning?" he asks.

"Being daunted to me, in our circumstances, brings with it a tingling within my soul. A situation so enveloping that it makes me feel complete. Whereas, what I felt prior to us revealing our feelings, while not empty, had lots of unoccupied space."

He puts his hand across, gently laying it on mine, and this slightest of actions sends my heart soaring. Concentrating hard, I continue, because what I have to say next, I believe, is important to his study.

"Picture me as a normal prisoner, an unaffected female," I say. "This envelopment, this complete lack of freedom, may absolutely devastate them."

"So, Janice Hutchings?" he says. "I have completely pervaded your soul, have I?"

That takes me aback a bit. "Aren't you concerned about my observation?"

"Not in the slightest," he says. "Realising that I'll need another, impartial subject to gather objective data long ago, this particular assignment is far too personal for such lofty aims."

I chuckle, lying back, nibbling on a vegan cheese and lettuce sandwich as I look at the gorgeous, cloudless, azure sky. Freedom—I so love it. Nevertheless, I'm in rapturous anticipation of what he has planned for me. The contrast is wonderfully, sensually provocative.

"I'm going to take you for a walk in his woods after we've finished here."

"Are you now?" I say. *After we've finished here* is deliciously lingering in my brain.

"Oh yes, on a leash, arms bound tightly behind, but not in prisoner mode."

"Isn't that a contradiction?" I ask.

"I can't bind you as a lover?"

Oh, fuck me. I'm no longer looking at the sky, back on my side, leaning on my elbow, peering at him as he smiles naughtily, displaying a hitherto unimagined side of himself.

"Is that what we are today?" I ask.

"I don't know, you tell me?"

You tell me? Taking his prompt, that's exactly what I do. Fucked if I know what's gotten into me. This greenhouse environment I've been under this last fortnight exaggerates my emotions as I move across, gently forcing him on his back and holding his wrists down while gazing dominantly into his eyes.

"Let me *tell you*, Gordon McGuire, that we're most definitely lovers. A situation I insist shall last forever, regardless of your wishes."

And with that, I lie on my back on the blanket once again, looking at the sky, while nonchalantly fiddling with the top button of my jacket with one hand as I nibble on my sandwich with the other. I suspect that all such privilege is soon to be removed by him, however, for the first time openly, truly — for the first time as my lover.

"You do realise you'll have to pay for such insolence, young lady?"

"Young lady?" I ask. "Is that your attempt to put me in my place?"

"Are you provoking me?" he asks. "Take care. It won't end well for you."

"Won't it?"

I'm expecting, hoping for him to come across and start playing with my tits and their ever-so-erect nipples. Instead, he goes to the van, promptly returning with a wooden mallet and four tent pegs, which he hammers into the ground beside me at once. They're spaced so as to obviously lay me out in my accustomed spreadeagled manner.

"Lie down with your arms and legs spread, my love."

The use of this term of affection, while quite enjoyable, hasn't the same gravitas as *prisoner* or *inmate*, but it emboldens me.

"Why should I?"

"Because I'm about to do several things to you that will have you, if not screaming, then certainly moaning with delight."

Moaning with delight? Time to stop all this parrying and thrusting, Janice. This is getting deadly serious. Doing as he says, I splay myself before him though feigning reluctance, even giving him a *humph* for good measure.

Ostensibly ignoring my protest—though I suspect he's feigning away, too—he then proceeds to bind me with his soft fabric thongs, such that I'm soon spreadeagled for his pleasure.

"So, dear lover, what is it you intend to do with me?" I ask.

"Nothing I believe you would readily expect, my child."

My child? With this and the promise of unexpected delights driving me to distraction, my heart thumps away like nobody's business—my stream of affection pouring from me.

He leans across, his hand heading toward my breast as I close my eyes in anticipation. However, his next move is both surprising and turning me on in equal measure. *He starts buttoning my blazer*—slowly, sensually, top button first, right down to the third. My eyes remain closed. Why in the fuck is this turning me on so much? And, even more importantly, how in the fuck did he know it would?

"Control, my love, control," he whispers, as though aware of my confusion, his face so close I can smell him. "*And* contrast. Me being able to do it and you so evidently unable . . .

the juxtaposition breathtaking, thrilling."

Jesus, Lord, almighty! Have I fallen on my feet here? Who would have imagined such romantic words — well, they are to me, and clearly to him — from such a studious man?

Scared to break the spell he's put me under, I keep my eyes closed as I sense his hand go under my dress. Oh, dearest Lord, how dare somebody so dominate another? How dare somebody snatch one's heart from its very chamber — one's soul from their very being?

With his fingers lingering close to my tormented vagina, he commands and coerces. "Open your mouth, child."

Open my fucking mouth? For what? So wanting to open my eyes, I squeeze them as hard as I can as I sense him put something in my very open, very willing gob.

A grape, a fucking grape. He's feeding me! He's fucking feeding me! Never has a grape's nectar tasted so sweet — be still my trembling clit, be still.

"I thought you might like me to do that," he whispers, his tongue sensitively licking my cheek, my ear, the back of my ear as his fingers enter me, explore me, then . . . *oh, Lord above* — he's beneath my dress.

"Hmm, what do we have here?" he asks, sensitively opening my flaps, exposing my poor little clitoris.

Poor little clitoris? Shut the fuck up, Janice. Do your worst invading ogre, don't listen to her, show it no merc — oh, fuck me dead.

The tip of his tongue barely touches, this slightest of contact invading, marauding my utter sexuality as he glides across, around, on — artfully, dexterously. I think I scream, not rightly sure. All I know is that it's entirely guttural as I cum like I've never cum before, in a visceral, earthly sensation that invades me with the ferocity of the most savage of beasts. How can such a tiny thing cause such a massive disruption? I pray that he'll stop — don't stop, don't you dare stop — certain that I'm about to be turned into a lunatic as yet again my body tenses before erupting. My mind, my soul, whatever, going apeshit once more as my head arches backward without a sound able to be uttered as I float into a heavenly paradise.

Coming to, for that's what it feels like, I look up to see his smiling face poking above my dress.

"Told you," he says before hurriedly untying my wrists, followed by my ankles

"Oh, yes, you did, my wonderful man, yes you did," I say, holding my arms out wide, beckoning him to enter. *Beckoning*? I must've read that in a fairy tale somewhere — a repressed memory brought on by extreme trauma. Chuckling inwardly at my droll observation, I smile as he responds accordingly, embracing me as only those in love could possibly know before gazing lovingly, hey, maybe even arrogantly at me.

"So, who's the master now?" he asks.

"I bow at your feet, kind sir, forever your idolizing slave," I say, smiling gloriously, adoringly. "Forget your restraints. Their grip has nothing when compared to your tongue."

"Forget my restraints? I'll do no such thing," he says. "As soon as we've finished our repast, fair maiden, you're to be bound, collared, and leashed as I guide you through the magic forest."

Together, we burst out laughing. Our unwitting jump into a medieval fairy tale all too much as warmly I embrace his strong body with my head leaning against his manly chest.

He has me collared and on a leash, but rather than him leading me, we amble side by side as lovers would on an affectionate stroll. The delicate chain of my leash hangs limply, purely symbolic, though still doing its job of inflaming my senses.

However, my bound arms are far from symbolic, with my wrists and elbows touching for the first time. This surprising act of brutality so inflames me that I find it difficult to concentrate on his interrogation.

"Why did you react so positively when I buttoned your blazer?" he asks.

"Purely because you did. The simple act of resisting the lure of my breasts, despite their vulnerability, showing that the power was entirely yours. And that I, *or* my body, no matter how tempting—had none."

"Remarkable, such nuance," he says. "This being dominated when bound further turning you on?"

"When dominated and bound by *you*," I say. "Don't forget how I reacted when Officer Manning did the same thing before leaving me alone."

"Yes, so you said, interesting that. Do you think it was mainly because it was her or because you were abandoned?"

"Both," I say. "I felt imprisoned in the police station, but my fear increased tenfold when she left me alone."

"I'm going to test that abandonment feeling today, my love. It's the main reason I brought you here instead of my garden. Its sheer size to increase your abandonment."

"Its sheer size?" I ask. "What have you got planned?"

"I think there's something going on inside you that we're not aware of," he says. "And I'd like to get to the bottom of it."

Something going on inside? Has Mother informed him of my repressed memory? As if. Mother exposing her secret self to anyone? I'm still surprised she told *me*.

Walking to a small clearing, he stops, eyeing a tall though slender tree. Its trunk is free from branches for its bottom three metres or so.

"This will do perfectly," he says, placing his backpack on the ground before opening its flap, revealing several neatly coiled pieces of light brown rope, one of which he takes in his hands, uncoiling it.

My heart immediately jumps with excitement as he tightly loops a double strand around me above and below my breasts, before cinching the bottom loop, which trusses my upper arms to my body. The rustic rope is in stark contrast to the refinement of my buttoned, tailored blazer. *Fuck me.* Is there nothing that evades my grasp — or his?

Next, he secures my lower arms to my waist, tightly cinching that double strand as well, and completely imprisoning my arms to my body before backing me up against the tree, which is basically vertical. Then, after tying and cinching my legs just above and below my knees and at my ankles, he fastens me to the slender tree with several double-strand loops — beginning at my neck and finishing with my lower legs.

But that isn't the end of it. Mind you, he needed no more, either to ensure my captivity or to heighten my arousal. By now, my moisture is flowing like a tap. Or so I thought. Filling my mouth with a flannel rag, he then wraps black medical tape around my face, covering both my mouth and eyes — the tape around both my eyes and mouth then further wound around the tree, imprisoning my head against it. Jesus Christ. This is the most immobile I'd ever been, even against the post when I had my first orgasm. Speaking of which, I reckon I'm only a nudge of his *magic* wand away from that amazing event happening again as I anxiously wait for his final touch to be applied.

"Of course you'll be expecting my *Hitachi* to be attached, my love. But that's not the point of the exercise. You may or may not have noticed in your excited state that I haven't plugged your ears. This is for a calculated reason. I want you to hear what's going on around you when I abandon you. I left something back at the van. Let's see, that's about an hour away, a two-hour round trip."

What? All of a sudden, I'm not so excited. I'm almost instantly panicking.

"So I'll be off then, darling. See you shortly."

And with that, he heads off. I can hear his footsteps getting further and further away as I try to let him know I'm not happy — in fact, I'm shitting myself at the thought of being left alone. But as I can barely move, it's futile.

CHAPTER NINE: A NAUGHTY GIRL FOUND

Janice

With Gordon's steps now out of earshot and my heart beating like billyo, I listen and smell to the best of my ability. Christ, I've never felt so vulnerable, with my breasts protruding as far as they can due to my loving master's cruel bonds. *Loving*? Even my ardour is stretched to the limit as I stand here listening for the slightest sound, such as the cracking of a twig beneath an interloper's feet or paws more likely. *Paws? Fuck me.* Thank heavens we don't have bears in our woods. What do we have? Hyenas? Dingoes? Not this far south. Perhaps a wild pig, though I couldn't imagine it rushing at me in my static state. No, apart from an inquisitive kangaroo, I reckon I'm right—snakes and spiders are as eager to stay apart from me as I am from them.

After thirty minutes or so of this anguished atonement, accompanied by not the slightest sound, I begin to relax, although I'm nowhere near returning to the aroused state I was before Gordon deserted me. Fuck, he's a strange one. It's clear he loves me as much as I love him, but he's quite prepared to leave me alone—completely vulnerable—all for the cause of science.

Thinking about this, the conclusions I reach begin to unwind me. If he loves me as much as I know he does, there's no way he would ever leave me in the slightest danger — and as he knows these woods, I reckon I'm okay.

Relaxing, I start thinking about the fun I would be having in this situation if he was still with me. Testing the bonds holding me against the tree, I push forward as hard as I can but achieve bugger all except to waste my energy, with the same result everywhere else — from my pretty blonde head down to my low-heeled, back-strapped dress sandals, yet again my urbane, tailored self is set starkly in contrast to not only my rough bonds but my rustic surroundings. Buttoned up and beautiful, imprisoned in the middle of the bush — how more contradictory and horny could that be? And with that delicious image in my brain taking over, my body in sync begins to completely relax. My vagina, while not weeping, is certainly warming to the task as the slightest of tingles rush through both it and my butterflied stomach.

A snapping of a branch! *Oh Jesus, Jesus.* Instantly terrified, I listen to my intruder's footsteps becoming louder and louder as they approach. Fuck me — could it be a deer? Or a goat? *A goat*? What the fuck, girl? Christ, what would I know? I'm a city girl through and through. Then it hits me. *Deliverance!* What if it's the deadliest predator of all — man? Some inbred hillbilly out hunting and finding me? Panicking at such a thought, suddenly an ominous, even threatening image of my mother flashes before me. Then disappears.

Fuck me dead.

But I've no time to reflect, have I? With my heart beating wildly, *it, she, he, whatever,* stands right next to me, seemingly inspecting me. *Dear God, dear God, protect me.* Expecting a hand or a muzzle against my overt breasts, for some reason, I start wondering why we women think of protecting them first, crossing our arms over them instantly if intruded upon. But *I* can't do that can I? With my thumping heart now accompanied by a sickening tremor, such as I feel when I'm close to the edge of a building, a further crushing of the leaves sounds — this one right next to me. About to faint, or so it seems, amazingly, astonishingly its footsteps begin to recede.

Dear God, thank you, thank you, thank you. I'll start going to church again, I promise, even the confessional booth, despite the fact my mob doesn't have one.

Suddenly I realised that a supreme being, if there is one, would see right through my empty promises. Clearly, my brain is telling me to relax. Well fuck that — I'm definitely not doing any such thing. I'm staying well and truly alert — with that snapping of the twig, the louder noise when he stood on the underbrush next to me, causing me to think it was either a booted human or a hoofed animal, but certainly not a paw.

And it's then that I think of Gordon, my beautiful, wise Gordon. He'll know what's going on.

An hour or so has passed since last I heard a sound. Suddenly, I hear footsteps — human footsteps — and coming from a different direction from the animal or whatever it was.

"Back, my darling."

It's Gordon. Thank Christ. I can't wait to tell him what happened as first he unwraps my blindfold, followed by my gag, which seems to take forever.

I splutter the cloth out as quick as I can, as well as my words. "Gordon, Gordon. You wouldn't believe what happened. I had a visitor."

"A visitor? Who? The Queen of Hearts? Alice? The Mad Hatter?" He chuckles. "There's nothing on his estate, darling. You don't think I'd leave you alone like that if there was?"

"Well, you're wrong," I say. "And it wasn't a visitor from through the looking glass either, smart arse."

About to begin untying me, he steps back, peering at me. "Who, pray tell, was it then?"

"Well, I couldn't tell, could I?" I ask. "They didn't untie me, did they?"

"As indeed mightn't I, if you keep spouting such nonsense."

I ignore him as — what the fuck? Back in his dominant but loving presence, miraculously, my moisture of joy has returned like a frightened bird once again sure of itself. *Jesus, bloody Christ*? Should I tell him? No. Bugger that, let's get this other bullshit over with first.

"All I can say is that it was either a human or a hoofed animal," I say.

"Well, since there are no such creatures on the estate, it must've been a human."

Suddenly, he looks alarmed . . . fearful. "What did they do to you?"

"*Do* to me? Nothing of course, or else I would know it wasn't some wild animal, wouldn't I?"

"So you weren't touched?" he asks.

"No."

As he's about to resume untying me, once more I stump him, all the while the glorious symphony of my bodily companion below accompanying me.

"I had a vision of my mother," I say.

Again, he steps back, this time staring rather than peering. "Jocelyn? When? And how?"

"Right when my intruder was about to touch me, or so I presumed."

"And what was your state of mind?" he asks.

"Well, what would you think, my darling? It, he or she, or they nowadays, was a stranger, about to violate me at my most vulnerable."

"So you weren't sexually aroused?" he asks.

"Are you insane? I was distraught, traumatised."

This seems to pique his interest. "Hmm, traumatised. You didn't seem so."

"*Seem* so?" I ask.

All at once he's laughing, clearly enjoying himself.

"You bastard," I say, though not with any great venom, glad to know it was him and to be in his adorable company once more.

Again, he steps forward to untie me.

"No," I say. "Now I'm like this, I need to be pleasured."

"Like *this*?" He gestures, indicating my captive body.

"That, yes, but more my aroused state," I say. "I'm in urgent need of some closure."

Chuckling, he approaches, with his body and handsomely rugged face right next to but not touching mine as he speaks. "One of two things can happen, my dear."

Oh God, his pupils are like moons again, and looking down as best I can, I can see he's physically invested. Is he going to take me like this? Untie my legs and give me a knee trembler? Thank heavens I wore my summer dress.

"Either I can attach something to you, which, as luck would have it, I happen to have in my backpack, fully charged. Or I could untie you and take you on the raw ground that lies beneath our feet."

"Seeing you've got a fat in your pants a drover's dog would be proud of" — I concentrate to maintain some level of composure — "I'm leaning to the latter. However, given the fact I'm also as horny as buggery due to my lengthy adventure, my answer is . . . both."

He chuckles. "*Both*, inmate? Aren't you the greedy one!"

With my head tilted to the side as best I can, I smile, viewing him amorously, cheekily, temptingly — words no longer needed to convey my desires.

"Heavens," he says, as he, too, smiles in response. "How could any man resist?" Then, he pauses. "I do, however, have one condition, inmate."

"A condition?" I ask. "Not that nonsense about me

requiring your permission before I cum?"

"As a matter of fact, no. Though now you come to mention it, I believe that's an excellent idea."

Me and my big mouth.

"*My* condition, however, is that rather than attach the said instrument to you, I shall hold it by your side. And both listening to and asking you questions throughout your various stages of arousal."

With my nipples and recently invigorated clit both seemingly as erect as humanly possible, I reply. My response, though, is more instinctive than intellectual with my inflamed state of mind. "Fuck me, that's asking a lot of someone about to explode."

"Is that right?" He smiles, switching his magic wand on at high speed — over my dress but precisely on my *button of love* as he'd recently described it. *Oh, for God's sake.* Clever bastard, when did he pick that bloody thing up?

"Now remember, inmate . . ." Fuck him using that term. He knows how much it turns me on when we're like this, informing him of this one lunchtime. I'll keep my mouth shut in future. This game of love is more tactical than life insurance, as I'm quickly discovering. "You must ask me for permission before cumming, *and* you must tell me what you're thinking as you progress."

Thinking . . . thinking? Fuck me — what the fuck am I thinking? About everything and nothing, all sorts of imaginings flash in and out of my brain as I answer to the best of my befuddled ability.

"You . . . you . . . no, my pussy, no you, no my fucked up brain . . . no you. Mother. *Mother?* Telling me I'm naughty, scolding me. *What the fuck?* You again, thank Christ. Your power over me. That's it, that's it, all I can think of, your pow . . . *uhh*, Jesus, Jesus, permission, sir! Permission!"

"No."

What? Is he insane? Something I'm soon to be if he doesn't give me the green light. How does he expect me to . . . oh, Christ, Christ.

"Permission, sir," I scream, cry, screech or whatever the fuck it is.

"No."

Fuck me! Is he pressing the thing harder against my pussy? *You bastard, you bastard, you fucking adorable bastard.* This expression of his power over me is driving me to tears, sensational, passion-driven tears as, eyes half open looking at the sky I plead softly, earnestly. *"Please*, sir, *please*, I beg of you . . . "

"What?"

Body writing in glorious agony, head bowed in utter defeat, I sob, my words of genuine anguish barely audible. "Please, master, please . . . release me from my torment."

"Go ahead . . . *prisoner*," he whispers, my entire spirit, or so it seems, bursting from within as simultaneously he savagely, passionately kisses me, his tongue invading not only my mouth but my mind, body and soul — my arms, in urgent need to embrace his beautiful body, struggling futilely against my, no, *his* bonds.

Oh, fuck me, fuck me, fuck me. What's just happened?

My exhausted, defeated body collapses, with my darling man frantically, urgently, releasing me from the tree before gently laying me face down as he continues to release me from his ropes.

With my head turned to the side and my eyes peacefully closed, I feel the raw blades of grass rub against the pampered softness of my cheek while he unties me, as I, once again, muse on the contrast of my highly civilised urbane-self thrust against my rustic surrounds. And as the contentment of my body progressively aligns with my peace of mind as Gordon slowly unties me, I doubt that a soul on this planet has ever been as happy as me at this present moment. *This* is heaven; forget that other place — nothing could be as serene as this.

Since I'm finished with my release, my darling tenderly rolls me over, lying on his side beside me and gazing longingly into my eyes.

"Someone looks happy," he says, smiling joyfully.

"Happy, yes, extremely so, but not as yet fully sated."

"Heavens," he says, seemingly astounded. "Such gluttony. What more could you ask for?"

"For you to take me, my darling. Softly, gently, as you've never taken me before. Clearly, you're in urgent need of my body. Have a look at the growth in your pants. In turn, I'm in urgent need of your caress, your *tender* love."

And with that, he lifts the front of my summer dress, leaving its underside to protect my delicate behind. Our eyes are never taken from each other's as his extremely hard member slowly, quietly enters me — the gentle rhythm of his thrusts certain to take me to, if not greater heights, then surely more serene ones.

Gordon

Strolling along, side by side, on our way back to the van, I've absent-mindedly taken her hand. Janice is welcoming it with a smile. It's such a lovely thing, this part of love, intimate companionship. I'd forgotten just how soothing it is.

"I want you to put on your psychologist's hat, darling?" she asks, jolting me from my daydream. "Explore why my mother's image came flashing into my mind. Something's going on there."

"Hmm, let's see. You have a repressed memory of an incident which your mother told you about."

"Actually, I have no memory of it. Whether that means it's

repressed, that's for people like Mother and you to decide," she says.

"If it's repressed, and we have no reason to disbelieve your mother, then that's usually caused by trauma. Trauma you said you were experiencing when I approached you in the woods."

"Yes. Right at that moment, she flashed in and out of my brain," she says. "And it wasn't just an image. It was a feeling, a sense of foreboding if you like, accompanying it."

I stop, facing her. "Foreboding? With your mother?"

"Well, I'm not completely surprised by that," she says. "We had the most toxic relationship until recently."

"Hmm, interesting," I say as we start walking again. "Was it the trauma of my idiotic game-playing?" She chuckles at that. "Or this toxic relationship with your mother that caused you to feel threatened by her image, or perhaps a combination of both. I'll need to do some research."

We reach my van.

"When we get home, I'll read the necessary literature. As it's your sexual release day, I have no need to tie you. What would *you* like to do? Read?"

"Read?" She stares, more or less glaring at me. "Dearest, I've finally discovered my libido, and let me tell you, that's at the centre of my thoughts. No, you do your research amongst your books. I'll do mine in the embrace of your loving bonds."

"*Bonds*? You want me to tie you up?"

"Gordon, I'm obsessed by it," she says. "The sensuality of being left alone in the woods was such a turn-on."

"Go on, this truly interests me."

"Can we re-create what happened to me today? Tie me to your post? At first, I was thinking in the nude, but today, when at my most vulnerable, as you secretly stood next to me, I felt completely exposed even though my blazer was buttoned up. Indeed, as *you* had buttoned it up."

"I like you like that," I say. "All neat and perfect."

"Rather than in the nude?"

"It's not an either-or situation, darling," I say. "I adore them both. Plus, I thought it would be a little twist. To do just the opposite of what you were expecting."

"Oh, yes?" she says. "And what was that?"

"To play with, perhaps even manhandle your breasts."

"Hmm, you're right on both counts," she says. "You did surprise me, and I was expecting you to play with them. Not manhandle them. You don't seem the type. A fair dinkum gentleman."

"Fair dinkum?" I ask.

"Yes. You're not putting it on. For example, I don't think you're turned on by the power of my captivity, more by how I look."

"My, who's being the psychologist now?" I ask.

"Am I right?"

Surprisingly, amid our extraordinary environment, I don't feel at all embarrassed by her probing and our ability to explore each other's thoughts urged on by our affection for each other.

"You are. I've always been super visual. Not superficial, because I can progress beyond that. In fact, I yearn for it . . . this positive feeling I'm experiencing with you. And I also had with Elizabeth, taking me to a marvellous place."

And with that, I take her into my arms, looking into her beautiful, light blue eyes. "I do truly love you, darling. I'm sorry for what I did to you today. I wasn't aware of your repressed memory situation, thinking it would be nothing but a delight to you being left alone with your thoughts, your sexuality."

"Oh, it was," she says. "As it will be later today when you leave me alone in the basement dressed as I am now, imagining all kinds of scenarios in my blindfolded state. Kidnapped by Indians, punished by an enemy, captured as a spy or by ISIS or whatever. My wicked, imaginative brain is taking me to all sorts of places."

"Exactly," I say. "Just as I was trying to create for you to-day."

"Yes, my love. But being left in your basement with you in the room above is a whole lot different to being abandoned in the wild."

What a delightful person she is — so much to explore. And then, with not a thought involved, I lean across and kiss her on the lips. Not passionately but fully, our lips entwining in a loving, affectionate embrace, the sweetest kiss of all.

"I love you, Janice Hutchings," I say. "Inmate supreme."

"Then prove it," she says. "Keep me buttoned up as you prefer. That, in itself, is a massive turn-on as it is you and not I in charge of my appearance. How dominant is that? Then tie me as tight as possible to that pole of yours and abandon me in your basement where I'll feel captured . . . discarded like a piece of unwanted furniture but secure in the embrace of your bonds, knowing you're protecting me above. How's that for a bag of mixed emotions, Mr psychologist?" She pauses, peering at me. "The important point, however, is to forget about my comfort. Save that for my diversion program. I want us to be full-on. Take me to my limits, Gordon, so I can see and feel what they are."

Wow. It takes bravery to be who you truly are, and this wonderful lady has got it in spades. And it's there, right at this moment — in my eyes at least — that we become fully committed and realise that this is not some dream but a full-on relationship.

"With the *Hitachi*?" I ask.

"Oh no," she says. "My captivity within your lovemaking rules, merely foreplay to you fucking me senseless in a few hours."

Holding her hand, I help her into the van. *My lovemaking rules? I wonder how long they'll last with you, my amazing temptress.*

CHAPTER TEN: DISCOVERIES ABOUND

Janice

Since my opening up to Gordon, our relationship has gone from the amazing to the sublime. And I love the framework in which we're operating. With me still his actual prisoner — Officer Manning's photos are an example of this for six of the seven days — and he sticking religiously to the rules. That's another thing about him I have come to adore — his dedication. He truly is a man of character, strong of conviction. And it's this strength that women admire in a man, not muscles, they're really only eye candy.

Plus, he's fulfilled my wishes, taking me to my limits while at the same time ensuring my safety. For example, his back-breaking hogties where he arches my back by attaching the rope running over my shoulders behind my neck to my ankles, with my safe words *thank you, sir,* letting him know when I've reached my limit. Christ, it's so tight I can no longer roll over to my side. And he never leaves me when I'm like this, despite my protests, gagging me tightly to actually shut me up, which further sends my mind and pussy soaring. Sometimes, he even puts me in a harness gag, pulling my head back to my elbows, which in these instances, are welded together at my insistence.

But the fact is, he's always right. For example, my safe *word* when gagged is the clapping of my hands, which occurs after thirty or so minutes at the longest. After which, he gently rolls me to my side, giving me instant relief, before leaving me alone to enjoy my captivity.

God, I love those moments — so strict but so peaceful, with my mind drifting off into *subspace,* as he informs me. And it is. Meditative, even. And something I could never do in real life, where my attempts at focusing my mind in silence for an extended period of time could best be described as lamentable. But here, lying comfortably on my side in the embrace of Gordon's skilfully placed ropes, my mind is completely at ease.

Although it isn't truly meditative, in the yoga sense, where you're trying to empty your mind. Instead, mine is purposely focusing on whatever drifts in there. Like the emptiness of my marriage to Rob, the happiness of my relationship with Gordon. But mainly on *this*, my extraordinary reaction to my captive state. Why am I like this? Is it nature or nurture? Surely it has to be the former? You can't really learn to love this. Perhaps learn to endure it. But to revel in it like I do?

A lot of it has to do with my OCPD, obsessive compulsive personality disorder — self-diagnosed I might add, I could never allow Mother to enter my mind — which, because it is viewed by its bearer as a positive in their lives can lead to amazing achievements.

Such as my successful career, or Rafael Nadal's or even Agatha Christie's character Hercules Poirot — as portrayed to perfection by David Suchet in that enchanting TV series, whose need for perfection I can so relate to.

But through all my daydreaming, the one thing I always come back to is Mother and that ominous feeling I had when left alone in the woods. So much so that I've become obsessed with it. I can't help myself, can I? Gordon, at my behest, has placed me in similar conditions in order to recreate the moment. And we've had partial success with her image quite often appearing.

But without the menace — which actually makes sense, as

she was the one who rescued me — the image more than often coming when I'm in a chair tie, as observed by my clever darling who is more than eager to explore this line of enquiry. But why *not* the accompanying menace I felt when alone in the woods? What's missing?

And then it hit me — trauma. And it's because of this revelation that I now sit here in one of Gordon's amazing chair ties. I've finally decided to go all the way. Left alone for twelve hours non-stop to see if I could return to the moment that Mother revealed to me just before my diversion program — where my father had lashed me to the chair as a child, depriving me of my senses.

I vividly recall the moment when I'd disclosed Mother's revelation to him, which I had to do to get him to agree to the drastic measures we're about to undertake — and his astonishing reaction. Early morning, I was in the shower, Gordon having just released me from my bedtime bonds.

"Before we begin, sir, I would respectfully like to ask you to indulge me in our endeavours today."

"Indulge you, inmate? In what way?"

"You recall two weeks ago when I asked you to purchase a full winter uniform from my old school, size ten, my size?"

"I do," he had said. "It's in the wardrobe waiting for you. I wondered at the time where that was coming from."

"Where it's coming from is that it was the clothing I was wearing when my mother rescued me from my father."

He slid open the shower door, clearly animated. "Rescued you? From what?"

"From the bonds that my father had put me in," I said.

"What the fuck, Janice?"

"It's okay, darling. It's had no effect on me. My memory of the moment is apparently repressed, according to Mother."

"And you never thought to tell me this?"

"No. Because it has nothing to do with my sexuality, the topic we've been exploring here."

"Don't be so sure of that," he said, appearing deeply concerned.

Turning off the shower, I'd taken the towel he handed me, drying myself.

"Mother says that repressed memories are usually associated with trauma, and my recently awakened libido is anything but that," I said, smiling knowingly at him.

"Yes, well, that was the same with a male client of Jocelyn's," he said, his concern still apparent.

"I know all about him."

"You do?" he asked, his apparent concern replaced by shock.

"Well, not his name or details, of course, just his circumstance. That he gets an instant erection when he ties a lady's hands."

"Like the sexual response you got when Officer Manning cuffed you," he hurriedly replied.

"Yes, but not in the police station. My sexual response is related to my sense of security, the love I'm feeling, such as with you."

"But you experienced this *before* you fell in love with me," he said.

"Oh yes, darling master," I said. "And when was that? From the moment you took charge of me, standing me at ease and barking at me like a drill sergeant? That's when I first became infatuated by you."

"Christ, that seems so long ago now."

"Twenty-five days, to be precise," I said. "But quite a lot has happened since then."

"Indeed," he said. "And all of it good, barring one regrettable incident."

"I'm not sure about that either. A great deal of good may

well come out of it. It was that trauma that brought Mother's image to the fore, the very same thing I want to recreate today."

"And how are you going to do that? There are no woods in this house, and the basement does anything but traumatise you," he said, chuckling.

"Very droll, master. But it isn't that scenario I wish to recreate, rather the one with my father."

Suddenly, he appears very solemn.

"Are you sure you want to do that? Your mother's patient hasn't, and apparently, he's as happy as Larry."

"Is he?" I asked. "How would you know that?"

"I just do. But that's beside the point. You may be opening up a can of worms here."

"Maybe," I said. "But unlike that weak prick, I don't want to live in ignorant bliss."

He seemed startled, probably by my bad language. But bad luck, I could be every bit as determined as he.

"Plus, unlike him, I've started to have recollections, especially that day in the woods."

"So, what's your plan?"

"I plan to dress in my school uniform and for you to tie me in the chair and completely deprive my senses, the way that Mother described, for the whole twelve hours today."

"The *whole* twelve hours?" he asked, clearly astonished.

"Yes, continuously. But not only that, not tied in your clever way but brutally, arms welded at the elbows, the lot."

"I'm not doing that," he said.

"Yes, you are, Gordon. This is very important to me. I need to know what truly happened."

"Twelve hours? Straight?" He paused, clearly thinking. "I'll have to look in on you every hour, make sure you're okay. I won't disturb you. You won't even know I'm there."

"Every four hours," I said. "I've already shown I can take

that. That's when you have to take your pictures for Officer Manning anyhow."

"Speaking of which, the time on the photos will show you've done the twelve hours consecutively."

"And you think she'll be worried about that?" I asked. "Quite the opposite, I reckon, taking delight in my mistreatment."

"Okay," he said, seemingly satisfied. "I'll go get your uniform, then, you can get dressed and have some breakfast. Get yourself well prepared for your persecution. For that's what it will be, trust me."

How brave we both were, leading to this strangest of moments, me sitting in the chair with my arms behind and over its back, barking out orders to Gordon rather than the other way around.

"Tighter, my love, at least so my elbows touch and my wrists. Then truss me to the chair so I can't move an inch, legs pulled back under me so my toes barely touch the floor."

On his knees before me, as he attends to my legs, he looks up, clearly exasperated. "Janice, please. I've done this before, you realise?"

"Of course, of course. It's just that I want you to be mean to me, and I know that's not your nature and how much you love me."

"More than you'll ever know," he says. "But don't worry, I'll be particularly strict. You'll be just as you wish."

"Thank you, darling," I say, as he goes behind me, completing my upper fastening.

"Right, done," he says.

"Is that it?" I ask. "You were very quick. You're not being nice to me, are you, Gordon?"

"Not in the slightest. Your crueller way is a lot easier than my more elaborate, caring method. That's why I sailed through it. Try to move."

Doing as he suggests, I can't.

"Fuck me. That's really tight," I say. "Thank you, my love. Let's hope it's all worth it."

"Yes. Well, your arms will become numb after a while, but not so that they'll be damaged. I've made sure of that."

He then picks up the cloth and black medical wrapping for my gag.

"Before you do, kiss me, my darling. I love you so much."

Gordon

"You do realise I have a master key?" It's Cathy, our house-keeper, after walking in on our latest *experiment*.

Having locked the study door where Janice was placed, I'm amazed she'd gone inside. "But my client has been placed in there for the last three and a bit weeks, and you've never entered before."

"Yes, I have," she says. "It's just that on this occasion, I thought you needed to know about Janice's state."

"*Janice*? You know who she is? How could you under all that covering on her face?"

"I'd recognize her tailored clothing anywhere," she says. "I have from the first day you got me to wash and dry-clean them."

"Recognize them? How?"

"I've been her housekeeper for years. Her's and Rob's."

Christ almighty, what were the odds?

"So what have you been doing all this time? Vacuuming and cleaning all around her?"

"Of course," she says. "She had no idea what was going on. The only time I had to move her was when she was on her side . . . her back arched to buggery. How can she take all that?"

I'm about to give her some lame excuse, but Cathy, in her typical no-nonsense way, sails on. "Anyhow, I just rolled her over onto her other side and vacuumed around her."

Rolled her onto her other side? Janice had never mentioned that. Oh, of course, her cryptic reference, *thanks for your help today,* the other week. So that's what that was all about.

"Don't be too worried about her *state* as you call it," I say. "She's not writhing in agony, God love her."

"I'm not talking about that," she says. "I realise what's going on there. She's in school uniform, for Christ's sake. No, she seems to be in distress."

Distress? My brave angel? Looking at the time on my phone, I see she's six hours in, part way through what would've been her second four-hour session. Fuck, with the stricter ties, I should've looked in on her every two hours, not four.

Bounding up the stairs three at a time, with Cathy following, I burst into my study, and there she is, clearly distraught, tearing my heart in two. Completely disregarding Cathy's presence, I tear at Janice's facial restrictions, revealing her crumpled, sweaty, tear-stoked face, the anguish in her eyes tearing me apart.

"Oh, Gordon, Gordon," she says. "It wasn't my dad, it was Mother."

"*What*? Jocelyn? It makes no sense."

Suddenly, she stops, noticing our interloper. "Cathy? What on earth are you doing here?"

"Gordon is one of my clients. I've been vacuuming around you for weeks. Only had to move you once."

"So it was *you* who rolled me over." She turns back to me. "Could this day become any stranger? First Mother, now this." She then turns back to Cathy. "What must you think of us?"

"I think nothing of you," she says. "It's none of my business or anyone else's. Client privilege uppermost as far as I'm concerned."

"You do realise I'm Gordon's prisoner?"

"I can see that."

"No. I mean his *actual* prisoner."

"Doubt you could get any more actual than this."

Sensing I'm needed, I jump in. "Janice is here under a magistrate-ordered thirty-day diversion program."

"And it's going quite well," Janice says, her distressing revelation about her mother seemingly put on the back burner for now.

"Is it?" Cathy says. "Anyhow, I'll leave you both to it. I've got a bit more to do up here."

And with that, she ups and goes, her cordless vacuum with her, leaving us alone.

"Oh, Gordon, what can I do?" Clearly, her horror has returned.

"*Do*? I would think that's obvious. You must talk to your mother at once."

"Gordon, don't you realise? At the moment, she's the last person I want to speak to. What I just remembered is chilling, frightening."

Going behind to untie her, she shrugs me off. "No. You know how it relaxes me. It's the only thing that's stopping me from losing it."

"Fine, fine," I say. I hold my hands open in mock fright before standing back, allowing her the time to collect her thoughts, which she clearly does.

Looking away, staring at nothing in particular, a solitary tear tumbles down her cheek.

Fuck this. I move across and sit next to her on an office chair, gently embracing her trussed body as best I can before leaning back and looking her in the eye.

"Tell me what you saw, darling. It will help you unload and give me a chance to analyse it all."

"Fine," she says.

Sitting back, I listen intently.

"Mother, she takes me into a small room. It might even have been a closet. No, it was bigger than that. Anyhow, she's talking to me, persuading me. *We're going to play a special game of hide and seek where you must be kept really quiet because the bogeyman's out to get you. Sit down in the chair, darling. Mummy's going to tie you in it so you can't move or make a sound.* Which then, she does. I'm not at all scared or frightened, even when I'm gagged and blindfolded. It's only when she puts the headphones on, the music cancelling out all sound, that I panic, but by then, I'm fixed to the chair. And that's where the image stopped."

"I have something to tell you, darling, something I believe your mother would also know by now, having received the same email. Knowledge I discovered immediately prior to the commencement of your diversion program. The reason I agreed to this twelve-hour session, which normally I wouldn't have done."

Seemingly sitting up even straighter in her chair, if that's at all possible, clearly she's all ears as I elaborate.

"There's a new study out. It suggests the best way to access hidden memories is to return the brain to the same state of consciousness it was in when the memory was formed. Apparently, the brain functions in different states, much like a radio operates at FM and AM. Tuned to FM to access our normal memories, it needs to be tuned to AM to access subconscious ones."

Janice's eyes are wide open, remaining mute as I continue.

"Without getting too technical, we have chemical receptors in the brain that control emotional tides. If a traumatic event occurs when these receptors are already activated in the brain, the memory can't be accessed unless the same receptors are once again activated."

"So that's why I was unable to recall my trauma. It was *physically* impossible."

"Exactly, my love," I say. "The brain is every bit as physical as the rest of the body, despite its intricate, complicated composition. So, whereas your mother's client is still unable to recall his past, he doesn't care. His mother's revelation, explaining to him why he gets an erection when he binds a woman's hands, exorcising him of all guilt."

"But he gets horny, not re-traumatised like me."

"And you don't get horny?" I ask.

"Well, yes, but I became distraught."

"Yes, when eventually you revisited the event, which he hasn't done."

"So, I shouldn't have revisited it?"

"But originally, that wasn't your doing," I say. "Officer Manning handcuffing you sparked your mind, your body reacting like your mother's patient in a sexual way. But you're right. He isn't actually revisiting it, is he? He's the one doing the tying, not the other way around."

She seems concerned, a furrowed brow appearing on her pretty face making her look even more appealing. God, I love this woman. However, it's not my love she needs at the moment but my counsel.

"So what happens when *he's* tied up?" she asks.

"The same thing apparently, as hard as ever. But it doesn't appeal to him as much. He has a dominant personality in the conscious world, so that prevails."

"Dominant? So that means I'm submissive?" She seems shocked. "Yet I'm highly successful in the insurance game, the toughest game of all."

"Firstly, all types of people like to play the submissive in sex games. Police officers, judges, captains of industry . . . all in roles of power in normal life. And secondly, don't confuse

toughness with strength, darling. For example, while men generically are stronger than women, women generically are
tougher than men, nature designing them to have our babies.
Can you imagine what would happen if men, given their god-
given mindset, all of a sudden had to give birth? Word would
soon get around the pub, *Don't be doing that man, it's murder.*
And it is. When asked to revisit the pain of childbirth, women
tell me of its intensity, one saying, *yet still I fronted up three
more times."*

"So it's not that we don't feel the pain as much, but that we
can take it better?"

"Exactly"

"So what are you telling me?" She pauses, smiling her gorgeous smile. "That, like my mother's patient, I should just enjoy myself? Especially since I've found the right man."

Smiling, too, instinctively, I lean across before gently kissing her on the lips. "I truly love you, Janice Hutchings. Your
cheeky, irreverent mouth that I constantly long to kiss. Your
beautiful face, your amazing intellect, your grace, your manner, your enchanting curves. And yes, even your kinky ways.
But *those*, not in a sexual way."

"So? I don't remember complaining the last time you made
love to me in your vanilla, missionary style," she says. "My
stuff's the entree, your stuff the main course."

"Main course? I like the sound of that, provided I'm forever
the chef. And as for your vanilla reference, let me tell you,
there's a lot more in the locker than that."

"Again, I couldn't care less. I'm so horny when you release
me, missionary's fine."

We chuckle.

"So, my darling Janice, what do we do now?"

"Do?" she asks.

"In relation to your mother. I think you must confront her,
discover the truth."

"Fat lot of good that's done me."

"But that's the point," I say. "You haven't found the truth, just a memory. You need to know the context behind it. Your mother, while as hard as nails, is the furthest person from a psychopath that I know."

"Exactly," she says. "Might be good at hiding it."

"But as you said, so what? We have to know the truth. We've got an exciting life ahead of us that could be ruined if we leave this lingering in the shadows."

As she stares at me, her face is awry, questioning. "You're right. Untie me, let's go."

"Go? Darling, we can't go now," I say. "We need you to finish your second four-hour session that you're supposedly taking. I have to take a photo. I'll ring her and ask her to come over here."

"Okay."

Finding Jocelyn in my contacts, I call her, putting her on speaker so Janice can hear.

"Gordon," Jocelyn says. "I was half expecting you to call."

"You were? Why?"

"I read the email about the subconscious memories, as I knew you would," she says. "So, knowing you and your obsessive ways, I suspected you might experiment with Janice, and return her to her trauma."

"Jocelyn, I'm in love with your daughter," I say. "There's no way I would do that. It was Janice, her memories drifting back when she was under extreme sensory deprivation —"

"*And* when she was tied in a chair?" she asks.

"How the blazes would you know that?" I ask.

"I'll explain it all when you both get over here."

"Over there? No, we can't," I say. "She's still under the diversion order. She breaks that, and she's in jail, her life ruined."

"Well, then, we'll have to wait until that's over," she says. "I have physical evidence I need to show her. Evidence I've kept in the safe for twenty-odd years that must never be made public, so there's no way it's leaving this house. How long has she left?"

"Three days," I say.

"Yes, well, good luck with that, knowing my daughter, she'll never wait that long."

Janice intervenes. "You're right, Mother. There's no way I'm waiting that long. See you soon."

And with that she indicates I should end the call, which I do.

Staring at her, it is clear the path she is going to take. What the fuck to do? Then it hits me. *Cathy.* Fuck me—as if. I could ask her, see what she thinks, and pay her double.

I call her on her mobile.

Janice stares at me. "Don't ring Mother again."

"I'm ringing Cathy," I whisper.

"Cathy?" Janice asks, seemingly amazed.

"Gordon?" Cathy says, answering her phone.

"Come back upstairs. I've got a job for you."

"A job?"

"I'll explain when you get here. Hurry, it's urgent."

Hanging up, I turn to Janice and start untying her.

"Cathy won't ever agree to it, Gordon. She's as straight as they come."

"Is she? How would you know?" I ask. "I happen to know she read *Fifty Shades of Grey.*"

"*Fifty Shades of Grey*?" It's Cathy, at the door. "What's that got to do with the price of fish?"

"We need you to take Janice's place for a while," I say.

"Her *place*?" Then, it clearly dawns on her. "Like that? No fucking way."

"Why not? Wouldn't you find it exciting?"

"Exciting? I'd go ape shit."

"But you read *Fifty Shades*?" I ask.

"So what? You men, you have no idea. It's not just about the sex. It's about how she thinks she can save him. It's a love story."

"I'll pay you double," I say.

"No way."

"Triple."

"No."

"One thousand dollars . . . cash."

"I said no. There's no chance in heaven I'm doing that."

"Ten thousand dollars?"

"Cash?" she asks.

CHAPTER ELEVEN: ARMCHAIR THRILLER

Gordon

After tying Cathy as cruelly as I'd tied Janice for the first photo, she sits in the chair wearing Janice's school uniform.

"Fuck me. That's tight. I can't move a thing."

"I know what I'm doing," I say as I reach across for her gag.

Looking down at her body, she says her last words for quite some time. "Lucky you were wearing a uniform, Janice. It's not waisted like your other clothes, so I can fit into it."

"How do you know you couldn't fit in my clothes?" Janice asks. "You're reasonably slim."

She scoffs. "With your hourglass figure? Besides, I tried on one of your jackets one day before I took it to the dry cleaners. Christ, your waist, I couldn't do it up in a fit."

I interrupt. "I'm about to put you into sensory deprivation, so beforehand, I want to be sure you know exactly what to do."

"*Do*? There's bugger all I can do like this," Cathy says.

"No, no. The point is I've set the camera timer for five. So don't move the chair an inch before then, as it's exactly in the right spot, and if the photo is slightly off, she'll notice, trust me. So, please, Cath, be brave and just sit there." I look at my phone. "It's three-thirty, so you've got one and a half hours to go till then. After that, you can do what you like, get undone if you can. Be a good test for my technique."

She stares at me. "As if." Then, she starts. "Hold on, you

said *after*. How long after? I don't want to be here all day. Even though I've organised my hubby to pick up our daughter after school, they'll still expect me home at some time to cook dinner."

Cook dinner? Fuck. "How about you ring him and tell him to get takeaways, and that you're *tied up* at work."

"Is that supposed to be funny?" she asks. "Gordon, I'm about to commit myself for up to three hours of extreme torment that may well send me troppo for all I know, and now you're asking me to extend it?"

"Twenty thousand?" I ask.

The look on her face — clearly, she's stunned. "Janice, get my phone from my handbag and hold it to my ear while I ring Shelton. Then you two nick off and leave me alone in my isolation while I think of what I'm going to do with my twenty grand."

Janice

As I stand with Gordon after ringing Mother's front doorbell, it's her, not Mary, who opens it.

"Come through, darling, Gordon," she says. "I sent Mary out to the movies or whatever, so the place is ours for a few hours."

She leads us through to the *parlour* as Mary calls it, asking us to sit, which we do, in separate chairs opposite her.

"So, where to begin?" she asks.

"How about with the evidence you were talking about on the phone," I say. "What evidence? And about what?"

Taking a deep breath, she looks me straight in the eye. "Your father was a monster."

"A monster? What are you talking about?" I ask. "Oh, fuck me, Mother, where are you going with this? Have I only remembered part of it?"

"No, no. Your memory of the incident with you locked away, tied in the chair, and with your senses taken from you is the extent of it. That's the absolute truth. But only because of the actions I took." She pauses. "Let me explain everything from the start to both allay your fears and give you the full context."

Gordon sits forward in his chair—as do I—putting his hand in mine, which I squeeze as Mother continues.

"Our marriage was everything I hoped it would be, your father the perfect gentleman . . . except for one thing. When he made *love* to me, and that's a euphemism if ever there was one, he turned into a monster, holding my wrists down and staring at me as if he was mad as he thrust at me until he came, and then, turning over as though everything was fine before staring at the ceiling."

"Are you saying he raped you?" I ask.

"No, no, darling. It was only in the final stages of our intercourse that that occurred," she says. "Nevertheless, I was horrified every time, hoping that side of him would not appear, but every time, it did. Long story short, I more or less got pregnant with you straight away, which gave me some respite because he wouldn't touch me after that. However, once you were weaned and my figure more or less returned, he wanted me again. I hated it even more the second time around. But seeing as it only happened for thirty-odd seconds three times a week, I put up with it. And though he never held you in his arms, he never once complained if you cried or interrupted us, just puffing on his pipe in the garden until you were asleep or quiet."

Tears were pouring down my face as I listened to my poor mother's plight, once again squeezing Gordon's hands ever so tightly.

As brave as ever, she continues. "Of course, being the

clinician I'm, I finally asked him what he was thinking about when he was like that? Was he thinking of me in a separate situation? Fantasising about hurting me?"

"For God's sake, Mother, you're so brave," I say.

"Naive, foolhardy more likely," she says. "Anyhow, turns out his fantasy was having me in the exact same situation that you ended up in."

"You mean bound and all the rest in a chair?"

"Exactly, but not in uniform, of course. So I suggested that rather than treating me as he did in the bedroom, which had ruined my taste for love, that he turn his fantasy into reality for thirty minutes, three times a week. And he agreed to it. We never had sex again, Instead, him pleasing himself or whatever he did as I sat there. He could have been jumping up and down for all I knew, as I couldn't see or hear a thing, thankfully."

She looks me square in the eye. "I suppose you're wondering how I could be so callous, but believe it or not, I was happy. To the outside world, we were a happy family, and as his profession kept him away most of the time, I, we, had little to do with him."

"His profession?" I ask. "What did he do?"

"He was an insurance agent."

I swear my heart has just stopped — only momentarily, but nevertheless stopped. However, I remain silent as Mother continues her horror story.

"He was a reasonably tall man and handsome, but I was so glad he was out till all hours. And those days, Mary wasn't on the scene full time, so nobody but he and I knew what was going on. So, save for my physical discomfort, I wasn't compromised, with life as perfect as it could be. Until the night that a show called Armchair Thriller appeared on the ABC."

"*Armchair Thriller*? What are you talking about? And when was this?" I ask.

"You were about five or six, going to school. It was one of the nights he was home for dinner and his fun and games with me after you went to bed . . . Monday, Wednesday and Friday like clockwork. I'll never forget it. This particular night was a Monday. It turns out the story on the television was about a young girl, I don't know, thirteen, fourteen, who'd been kidnapped and was held for ransom. In a navy uniform like yours, she was kept in a chair, blindfolded, and gagged with headphones on. At the time, I thought nothing of it, as I did right up until the Tuesday after the last of the three episodes of the thriller had been aired. And then, out of the blue, he calls me late afternoon and tells me he wants to have a serious talk with you before dinner and, I'll never forget his words, *I want her in her uniform.* Again, this didn't ring any alarm bells. I mean, a serious talk, perhaps he wanted you to be dressed appropriately, I don't know. It was odd, I admit, but never did I suspect what was going on."

"When *did* you suspect?" I ask.

"The same day," she says. "Mary was off duty. So it was just you and I, and you were reading a book in your uniform as I'd asked you to be while our dinner was cooking. So I went into the study to get my own psychology book when I noticed a drawer on his bureau that he always kept locked was slightly ajar. Curious, I went across to push it back in, but it wouldn't budge. Strange, I thought and pulled the drawer out. and hanging down from above was the end of a file."

She pauses, looking at us both as though ensuring we were paying attention. *Paying attention?* Never have I been as enthralled.

"At first, I thought, this is none of my business," she says. "But then intrigue got the better of me, and I opened the secret compartment. Thank heavens I did. In it was a file full of paper clippings of a serial abductor who was terrorising the suburbs of Melbourne at the time, taking young teenage

119

schoolgirls and releasing them after a few days. And with it a small tin which I opened up, and inside there were five or six locks of hair with a small ribbon tied around each."

Horrified beyond belief, I rush over and take her into my arms. "Oh, Mother, you poor thing. What must you have been thinking?"

"I can tell you exactly what I was thinking. You," she says. "Picking up the files, I rushed downstairs, knowing he was only twenty minutes or so away, and that's when I hid you away."

"Hid me away?" I ask.

"Yes. Mary had shown me a large cupboard, or room, under the stairs that I never knew was there, which she used to put her cleaning utensils in — locking it up afterwards so you wouldn't even notice it. I knew he wouldn't know about it, so I put the file and you in there, using the belts and other stuff he used on me, which I'd taken from another drawer in his bureau. I knew I couldn't take the risk you would keep still, so that's why I restrained you. I'm so sorry, darling, but I was desperate."

Brushing her hair with my hands, never have I been so proud of another human being. "You have nothing to be sorry for, dearest Mother," I say. "But in my memory flashes, I never felt in danger."

Which wasn't exactly true, but it was near enough.

"No," she says. "That was because I made it out to be a game, that the bogeyman was coming, and we had to keep you still, quiet, deaf."

"So what happened next?"

"That's when the tough, uncompromising me first came to the fore," she says. "When he came home, I confronted him. Told him you were at a friend's house and that the evidence of his infamy was now under lock and key in a solicitor's office. Sealed for now and as long as you and I remain unharmed and he was out of the country. At first I thought he was going to kill me, but I stood up to him, looked him square in the eye. *Go on,* I said, *and then all your photos and locks of hair will be all over the news.* Well, like all bullies without power, he went to water, rushing into the study to check that his precious goodies were truly gone before packing a bag.

"*You've got twenty-four hours. Now fuck off, you freak,* I said."

I don't know why, but I start laughing, staring at her in amazement. "I can't imagine you speaking like that."

Mother, too, chuckled. "I've never said that crude word before or since. But I did then, and I meant every vowel and consonant of it. Anyhow, that's exactly what he did. And I haven't heard from him since."

Sitting on the arm of her chair, I'm in rapture of her. "Don't you see, Mother? That's why it wasn't a trauma to me. You turned it into a game. Unlike that poor man, your former patient, whose parents traumatised him."

She smiles before turning to Gordon. "Speaking of whom and as we're revealing all, isn't it time you spoke up, Gordon?"

Gordon has turned as red as a beetroot. *What the fuck?*

"What? Er . . . I have no idea what you're on about, Jocelyn," he says.

"Is that right, Gordon McGuire? Former *patient* of mine."

Patient? And then it hits me. Fuck me dead. *Gordon?* The mystery patient?

With a furrowed brow, he peers across at me. "It doesn't change anything, Janice."

"Change? Of course not. Why would it? I love you, and you love me," I say.

"That's not what I meant. I mean, as far as our sexual arrangements are concerned."

Mother intervenes, smiling at Gordon. "*Sexual arrangements?* Have you been taking advantage of your patient's

121

vulnerability, Gordon?"

"No, I have not, and you know I never would," he says.

"*Know*?" I ask. "What does he mean, Mother?"

"Gordon is suffering from the delusion that he was the cause of his wife's demise."

"As I was," he says.

Even though I'm partly aware of what they're talking about, I'm still confused. So I shut the fuck up, allowing these two to sort it out alone.

"Gordon, your darling Elizabeth's cervical cancer was not the result of her taking the pill."

"Yes, it was, and it was me who insisted she take it. I wanted sex with her every day. Tie her hands, then lay her down."

Now I interrupt. "*Tie her hands then lay her down*? It seems that you've changed your ways, darling."

Turning to me in apparent surprise as if he'd forgotten I was there—probably had, the obsessive bugger—he's forthright. "And that's the way it will remain. Contrary to what your mother says, the contraceptive pill does contribute to cervical cancer."

"*Does?* Gordon, or *can*?" Mother asks. "Let's see now, if memory serves me right, it's a ten per cent increased risk if you've been on the pill less than five years and sixty per cent between five and nine years."

"But I have no intention of going on the pill, Gordon," I say, grabbing his attention again.

"You don't?"

"Of course not. I've had an IUD inserted in my uterus," I say. "Not that it seemed to worry you too much."

"Worry me? Heavens, I'm not sure I was thinking of anything other than your beautiful self at the time," he says. "I hope you don't feel the lesser of me, my darling."

"On the contrary," I say. "As you said, you're *all or nothing*

122

at all, and that proves it, that you're happy to have children with me. That means a lot to me."

"It does? You want children?" he asks.

"With you, undoubtedly. But that's not my point. It's the fact that you weren't concerned. Our love was more important than such matters."

He smiles, no he grins, clearly about to reply, but I haven't finished.

"But that still doesn't explain to me why you won't have sex with me when I'm bound."

"I vowed after her death to control my urges, which I blamed for her death." Mother is about to say something, but he stops her short. "I use the word *blamed* in the past tense, Jocelyn, so don't get on your high horse. I realise, at worst, it was a minor point as she wanted sex as much as me, possibly more." He turns to me, smiling. "As indeed does your lovely daughter. With us, however, my darling, it's more the doctor-patient relationship that holds me back. As Jocelyn said, *taking advantage of your vulnerability.*

"So you think you'll be able to have intercourse with me when I'm helpless after the program finishes?" I ask.

"Oh, I know I will."

Well, there you go, I was right. His dilated eyes, his excessive attention to my attire — he did have a fat, the bastard.

Mother interrupts. "You better get back to your home before you're discovered by that manic policewoman. She'll have you locked up before you know it."

I stare at Gordon. "Cathy!"

He looks at his phone. "Let's see, she'd have had her photo taken. It's an hour or so back to Yarra Glen. She'll be fine. Earn her money."

"I won't even enquire about who this Cathy is," Mother says. "But what about Rob? When do you plan to tell him about your love for Gordon? It's going to break his heart."

Christ, what with all this hullabaloo, I hadn't thought about that. "I'll tell him tonight, as soon as we've done what we have to at your country hideaway, Gordon, which I now know is Yarra Glen."

"You're welcome to know, indeed, as you're welcome to know all about me. There will be no secrets between us, my darling."

Chapter Twelve: Curses! Foiled Again!

Janice

Right, one problem solved—Mother. Cathy, she's currently being untied by Gordon in the study, which, as he said, is *his concern, not mine*. Implying, of course, that the next problem, telling Rob it's over in a manner that doesn't shatter him, is entirely mine.

Cathy, now back in her own clothes, enters the room with Gordon, a smile on her face the Cheshire Cat would be proud of.

"Why so cheerful?" I ask.

"Gordon just transferred the twenty grand into my bank account," she says.

"Good on you," I say. "You earned it, helped us out of a spot, kept me out of jail. Unfortunately, I doubt you could help me with my next problem. How to tell my husband I'm in love with another man."

"Oh? And when do you plan to do that?" Cathy says.

"Right now. My evening four-hour session is about to commence, so Gordon can rig me, take the photo, and we can be back in time for the end-of-session photo."

"Sounds like a plan, but I wouldn't be doing that if I were you," she says.

"You wouldn't? Why not?" I ask.

"Officer Manning will be there."

"Officer Manning? How would you know that?" I ask. "In fact, how do you even know her?"

"Since you've been locked up, she's been staying there overnight," Cathy says. "Usually arriving after five."

Officer-fucking-Manning — and Rob? I sit down.

Gordon jumps in. "We need a new strategy, darling," he says, before turning to Cathy. "Thanks for what you've done, Cathy, and for the heads up, we owe you."

"Thirty thousand?" she says jokingly, or at least I think it's a joke.

Gordon chuckles. "We'll take it from here, my friend. Don't let Rob know you know me."

"It'll cost you." She again jokes — I think.

"It's only funny once, Cathy," he says before escorting her to the door.

"Okay, okay. But if you need me to fill in for Janice again, I'm up for it," she says as she leaves.

Returning to me, Gordon manages a smile. "I think I know what we can do."

Rob

I'm down below under the sheets, pleasuring Officer Manning, when my phone suddenly rings.

"Fuck me," she says. "It's Janice. What the fuck is she doing? She's supposed to be locked up."

Scrambling to the surface, I grab my phone, staring at her name. "I better answer it."

"You *think*? Put her on speaker."

I nod and then press the answer button. "Janice? What's going on? I thought you'd be tied up, literally."

"I have something important to tell you. I'll see you in an hour."

And with that, she hangs up.

"An hour?" I stare in wonder at my curvaceous angel. "What do you think that's about?"

"Who the fuck knows?" she says. "But I've got to get out of here. I'll park a block or so away, then as soon as she arrives, call me."

"Call you? Why?" I ask.

"So I can nab her. Lock her up."

"We've discussed this," I say. "That's not going to happen. Bad enough we've put her through this torment without ruining her life."

"Torment? I'm not so sure about that," she says. "She's been getting her sexual relief every week. So something's going on."

"Going on? Between Gordon and her?" I ask. "Don't be fucking stupid. I told you, she's an ice maiden."

"Hmm. All right then. But if you find out otherwise, ring me, and we'll put the bitch where she belongs. Meanwhile, I'll fuck off to the nearest *McDonalds*, and you can call me either when she's gone or if you change your mind."

"Yeah, yeah," I say. "Off you go, darling, go keep that beautiful figure of yours in prime condition with some prime Angus beef."

"Exactly," she says, adjusting her belt and putting her cap on before kissing me gently on the lips. I love it when she does that. It shows her affectionate side.

The hour passes, more or less, when the front door opens and in walks Janice. She's well-groomed with not a hair out of place—and as cold as ever.

"Hi, darling," I say, kissing her on the cheek.

"Rob, dearest, I have something to tell you," she says. "It's very important. I think you should sit down."

"Sit down? I'm fine, Janice, just say what you have to say.

I'm sure it's not as bad as you think."

"I'm leaving you," she says. "I'm in love with Gordon."

"You're what?" *Fuck me dead. What irony.*

"I'm sorry. I know it's probably breaking your heart, but I think it's best for the both of us. I'm just not able to respond to you as I do with him."

"Respond? With Him? What the fuck are you talking about?" I ask. "You're as frigid as an ice block."

"Not with him, I'm not. I get as horny as buggery when he ties me up. Love being his captive."

"Is that fucking right?" I've never been so pissed off. "Well, if captivity is what you're after, I've got just the thing for you."

Grabbing hold of her arm, I call Officer Manning.

"Stop it, Rob, you're hurting me," she says. "Who are you ringing?"

"Officer Manning. She'd love to see you," I say.

"Officer Manning? But, Rob, I thought you loved me?"

"*Loved* you? You wouldn't know what love is, you silly bitch. I fucked you, Janice, fucked you, that's all." I hold my arm around her neck to quieten her down, and my darling finally answers the phone.

"Fuck, what took you so long? Are you getting one with the lot?"

"Fuck off, Rob," she says. "What's going on?"

"You were right. I've got the cheating slut here, waiting for you to take her into custody."

She hangs up. Putting the phone away, I take Janice across to an armchair, forcibly shoving her into it. "Sit there and behave yourself. She's only a few minutes away."

"A few minutes away?" she asks. "I don't understand?"

"Understand? Of course you don't understand, you loveless bitch," I say. "Officer Manning and I are in love. Have been for ages. We set you up. Thought you'd be picking up garbage for a year or two, giving us time together to see if we were fair dinkum or not. Then your mother came up with this Gordon idea, which threw a fly in the ointment, or so we thought. But actually, it was better, gave us a chance to live together, and we love it."

"Wait. So hold on, you and Officer Manning entrapped me?" she asks.

"Did we what!" I say. "She wanted to lock you up, fair dinkum, which I wouldn't agree to. And then she came up with this diversion program bullshit. I've changed, though. Now I'm happy to see you locked up, your professional life ruined."

"But, darling, don't you see?" she asks. "We've both got what we want . . . happiness."

Just then, the door opens, and in walks my voluptuous darling, brandishing her handcuffs. "Stand up, you bitch, I'm taking you in."

Janice stands and turns before placing her hands behind her, smiling as she allows herself to be cuffed.

"She's smiling," I say.

Officer Manning turns her around, inspecting her. "You've got nothing to be happy about, bitch."

"Yes, I have," she says. "I know that you and Rob entrapped me."

Officer Manning turns to me. "What did you say, you stupid bastard?"

"Who gives a fuck?" I ask. "She can't do a thing. It's her word against ours."

"You fucking idiot. We're having an affair, if you haven't noticed. Don't you think that will give her story some weight?"

"Why did you and Rob entrap me, Officer Manning?" Janice asks. "There was no need. I would've been fine with it all. You and him."

Uh oh, I've seen that look in my curvaceous darling's eye

before—she's about to lose it. I begin to say something, but she's off and gone.

"*Entrap you*? You want to know why?" she asks, her cheeks aflame, her voice raised. "Because you and your like at school, the perfect, little, skinny bitches, gave me buggery. So yeah, I entrapped you, couldn't wait to see you get yours. I've done it before to similar types, but this? This is so much sweeter."

"Have you got all that, Gordon?" Janice yells.

"Sure have, darling," Gordon says, tapping the keyboard on his phone as he enters the room. "Just sending it off as we speak."

"Gordon!" I say. "How in the fuck did you get in?"

"I do happen to own part of this place, Rob," Janice says, her hands cuffed behind, and Officer Manning gripping her arm.

"You stupid bastard, Rob." Officer Manning says. "Now *we're* the ones that are fucked."

"Not necessarily," Janice says. "We have something on you. You have something on us. Take these cuffs off, and we'll sit down and talk."

Clearly, my Rubenesque partner is none too happy, but reluctantly, she relents, taking Janice's cuffs off before we sit down opposite each other, my pissed-off angel and I in separate armchairs, with Gordon and Janice hand-in-hand sharing a settee.

Janice opens proceedings. "Gordon and I will keep our recording of your joint confessions," she says before turning to me. "You're so easy to read, Rob. I knew you would react that way, your heart leading your head as per usual." She then addresses my darling. "And, as for you, Officer Manning, your chip on your shoulder is as obvious a marker as could be. You really should do something about it."

"Fuck you, bitch. This isn't all over. I'll follow you everywhere. You'll slip up, jaywalk, something like that."

"Why do you think Gordon and I will keep your confessions?" Janice asks. "Exactly to stop any such bullshit. But it doesn't have to be like that. As I said before, I've got Gordon, and you've got Rob. You can move in here. I'll move in with Gordon."

"What? Are we doing a property settlement?" my darling asks.

"Are you happy with that, Rob?" Janice asks me.

"Absolutely. I'll buy you out, and my cuddly darling can move in permanently." I turn to her. "Are *you* happy with that, my love?"

"I suppose so," she says. "Pissed off I'm not locking her away, though."

"Don't worry about that," Gordon says. "I'll make sure she's secure. Speaking of which, we still need to take today's final photo. I take it you email it on to the magistrate, Officer Manning, so it's important to you, too."

"Yes," she says. "Fuck off and do that, and for the rest of her sentence."

"Have no fear, she'll be doing that," Gordon says. "Indeed, her final sexual release is tomorrow."

"Ugh, too much information," my darling says. "But *don't* forget the final two days and the photos. By the way, is that what you've been doing all along? Taking a photo at the beginning and one at the end, in between sitting down and having a cup of tea and a chat?"

Janice replies, taking Gordon's arm and smiling lovingly at him. "And deny myself the pleasure of his restraints?"

"So you get off on it?" my darling asks.

"With him, yes . . . but not you."

Astounded by this, I jump in. "So you've become sexually responsive?"

"With Gordon, absolutely," she says. "But don't take it personally, Rob. I'd never been restrained before, and I've got you and Officer Manning to thank for that. Despite your ill intentions, you both opened up my world for me. Thank you very much."

Chapter Thirteen: Truth Revealed

Jocelyn

Sitting in the cafe with Mary, we're joined by Julie, aka Officer Manning, who, upon espying us, comes across.

"Good evening, Jocelyn, Mother."

"Good evening, my darling child," Mary says. "We're both very happy with you, aren't we, Jocelyn?"

"Absolutely," I say. "It turned out perfectly. Rob falling for it hook, line and sinker."

"I'm so glad you're happy with me," Julie says. "Can I sit down with you both?"

"You may," I reply.

As she sits her fat arse down, I set the ball rolling. "So you're certain Rob has no idea of our collusion?"

"None whatsoever," she says.

"And you're happy to keep up your charade with him?"

"That's what I wanted to talk to you about. It's no longer a charade. I love the silly bastard."

Fuck me. I hadn't thought of that, which now I do with Julie clearly sweating on my response. "As long as it doesn't interfere with any future plans, it's fine," I say. "No doubt we'll find someone else's world we can manipulate, wouldn't you say, Mary?"

"Whatever, Jocelyn, you're the boss," Mary says.

"Exactly," I reply. "I went to a lot of trouble to get you on the force, Officer Manning, the two of us with so many adventures ahead of us."

I'm happy to call her by her official title as it fits in nicely with her delusion of grandeur. The stronger she thinks she is, the better for me, with her position of power being extremely useful. Her body-shamed inferiority complex, on the other hand, ensures she's only one serious setback away from becoming the girl I started treating when she first came into my life.

"You two may leave now," I say. "Off to your movies. I have so many things to think about."

And indeed, I have. A brand-new female patient with extreme depression has entered my life, and she'll be like putty in my hands, just as Gordon and Janice and Mary and Julie have been. Watching them leave, chatting away like mother and daughter—I wonder what that's actually like.

As I sit back and relax with my pot of Earl Grey, taking time to reflect; my solitude allows me to meander through my thoughts without a filter, something my controlled life rarely affords me.

It's not that easy being a psychopath. People don't understand us despite our plight being graphically illustrated in that marvellous biographical epic, *The Silence of the Lambs*. And by graphically illustrated, I'm not just referring to the scene where the hero, Hannibal Lecter, bites into the neck of a victim while attached to a heart monitor, all the while displaying no rise in his heartbeat even though he appears to be passionately enjoying himself. That's just it. We don't *passionately enjoy* anything, as it is our minds rather than our hearts that are engaged.

And it's this cerebral dexterity of ours—delightfully exhibited by Hannibal through his relationship with his *emotional* victim Clarice Starling—that's the even more illustrative, satisfying part of the movie for me.

How he could sense her attraction to him and use it to manipulate her. The moment when their fingers touched through the bars was psychologically thrilling to me, as I imagine the most tender of love scenes would be to the rest of the human race.

I never use the word *normal* when referring to the rest of the population. Such a term is the ultimate in homogeny, classifying all humans as being uniform in structure or composition. As I told my daughter, the very fact we literally have to learn everything that makes us who we are is testimony to the falsehood of this concept of normality. Heavens, we all have different upbringings, experiences, parents, friends, extended family, and acquaintances that influence our destiny. This makes each human being unique — indeed, precious — with our *inherited* instincts, aka our nature, infinitesimal when compared to our *learnt* ones.

I use the analogy of the earth and its atmosphere, our sky, to illustrate this point. When seen from space, it is the tiniest, thinnest of layers. However, it's of vital importance to us. Yet, just as we humans take our sky, the air that we breathe for granted, so too do we view our inherited nature. disregarding it except in our art forms, like our movies, with phrases such as *may the force be with you* in *Star Wars* chilling in its insightful accuracy.

Dear Lord, there I go again, straying from the point and going off on a tangent which this wonderful, detached mind of mine so encourages. I wonder what I, or any psychopath, would be like with dementia? With our filter, stronger and more necessary than most, no longer there to protect us — hide us. Now that would be a most interesting study.

But back to where I was. How difficult life is for a psychopath, especially a practising one like myself. Firstly, what to do with one's life? For me, this lack of empathy for my fellow human beings led me to study psychology, a dry subject if ever there was one. Indeed, my lack of emotion makes me the most objective psychoanalyst imaginable.

This choice was initially undertaken for two reasons. One, to give me a greater insight into the human mind in an attempt to ignite this empathy — futile, as it turned out. And two, to give me the opportunity *to change people's lives* as I so proudly announced at my initial interview with the university head — if only he, and I at the time, knew.

You would think operating a psychology practice, given the insight into people's lives it provides, would make manipulating these lives easy — it doesn't. These constant mishaps to my daughter don't just miraculously occur. Careful, forward planning is what is required, some precise, some not so much. For example, at the outset, Officer Manning informing me the moment she pulled Janice over that morning, ensuring I was there at the police station to *rescue* her in her hour of need — that was entirely precise.

On the other hand, after getting her name from a colleague, recommending Cathy to Gordon before getting Mary to further recommend her to Janice — not knowing for sure where it would lead. Or getting Officer Manning to encourage Rob's advances, again vague about where it would lead, but certain it would, at the very least, complicate Janice's life.

However, my piece de resistance was introducing Officer Manning to Magistrate Thomas, a colleague of mine at my club, and knowing how compatible they would be as far as law and order is concerned. Thomas, in particular, wanting to come down hard on wealthy offenders who he believed were *rorting the Diversion Program system.* It's a view I knew would dovetail perfectly with Officer Manning's own hatred of these *middle-class, entitled bitches.* So, after getting her to conspire with Rob to entrap my daughter, I knew exactly where she would be heading — to the diversion program. The reformative, left-wing program tailor-made for Gordon's so-called *penal reforms* happened to reconcile with Officer Manning's and Thomas's conservative views. There's no way in hell any other authority figures would have gone near them, but I knew they would. All this taking place as I continued to encourage Gordon's twisted logic — well aware that his fetish for bound women, whether he realised it or not, was the true driving force behind his crazed reforms.

The result of all this was that I was now armed — through the diversion program and Gordon's accompanying penal reform — with the perfect vehicle for any of my future patients to be tested to their limits, even though it had all started with just my daughter in mind.

Speaking of whom, her revelation that she *felt a tingling warmth in my nether regions* when cuffed by Manning, while at first seen by me as a negative, soon came to be seen as an interesting development. Indeed, the prospect of two people with a similar experience that seemingly had produced a similar fetish becoming involved romantically — salivating, to say the least. Especially considering the fact that I'd advised Gordon to disassociate any future sexual activities from his bondage fetish, this too certain to complicate matters for our star-crossed lovers.

I first met Mary in the labour ward where I was supposedly suffering from post-natal depression — though I knew better. Instead, my psychopathic, narcissistic self was pissed off, wondering how in the fuck I'd got myself into this mess. How I'd allowed that fucking little bitch of a baby to ruin my once perfect body — swearing to myself that someday, someway, she would pay for it.

Mary, though, she was just the opposite. She was distraught about having to give her brat up for adoption. Once an orphan herself, she was penniless and about five years younger than me, and we more or less hit it off instantly. Not in the true sense of the phrase. I'm not, nor ever have been, capable of friendship, more or less copying other people. Just as I had when *falling in love* with and marrying Janice's father before bearing his fucking child—and look how that turned out. Still, he didn't last too long in my life, Janice's incident putting paid to that little experiment.

But back to Mary. I'd set her up in her housekeeping business—the only thing she knew how to do, having done it all of her life in the orphanage. However, this time she was getting the wages she deserved. Cutting out the middleman, I, and a few of my acquaintances, had used her more than competent services before I finally became her full-time employer. She's a bloody good worker, I'll give her that. And due to her vulnerable position at the time, she was especially malleable, enabling me to fashion her into the closest thing I had to a friend because, basically, she was my slave.

I'd even turned her naturally happy disposition into one where she distrusted the world, happy to assist me in my endeavours. And then, when her daughter came into our lives with Julie tracking her mother down, I encouraged Mary to accept her, indeed love her, in the hope it would give me two slaves. Which it did, allowing me to immediately manipulate Julie after discovering the huge chip on her shoulder. Then, I'd used everyone and every trick I knew to get her into the police academy, where she surprised us all, hauling her fat but strong arse through her training, clearly having inherited her mother's work ethic.

She's happy now in her position of power with me throwing her a few bones along the way in the form of patients whose private disclosures I'd used to their disadvantage. For example, Marilyn Hughes, a closet kleptomaniac. As rich as one could imagine and pretty to boot, I knew her very existence would rub Julie up the wrong way. I had Julie follow her in plain clothes before nabbing her on the street. No diversion program for her. Instead, a five-year custodial sentence with Officer Manning presenting her to the court as a *privileged female who took pleasure in her thievery and her victims' losses*—also citing to the court her long history of shoplifting, which I'd passed on to Officer Manning, offences that Marilyn had confessed to after much pressure from the oppressive policewoman. I was happy to give her these pickings, knowing she would one day pay me back in kind for my pet project—my darling daughter, Janice.

The loathing I felt toward her after her birth for ruining my once perfect body—which she then had the cheek to inherit, the little bitch—forever stayed with me. And I purposely made life hell for her, creating this buttoned-up individual with no friends—why should she have them, I don't—who had then run from me as soon as she legally could. I, however, had astonished her by generously buying her a flat and giving her a substantial bank balance, interested to see how she'd go given the mindset I'd given her.

These manipulations had surprisingly turned her into a tough-as-nails hard-arse—a hard-working, respectable sociopath, which most captains of industry are. with her hardened, tough soul and pretty charms enabling her to manipulate people while making herself a fortune. One might even say a chip off the old block.

Shit I nearly felt pride then.

Hardly. That's an emotion, something I never actually feel—just sense what I think it would be like. Like when I cried with Janice, my hanky at the ready to use so that when she looked at me after our embrace, I was wiping my eyes, no tears to be seen. A trick I'd learned from a TV interview with a famous actress I'd viewed.

Janice, on the other hand, she has true emotions—hence her downgrading to a sociopath, though it must be said at the lower end of the scale. In fact, she's a lovely person, which is good, making her as manageable as the rest of the population—perfect for exploitation. That's the thing about human beings. They're communal. Born with an urgent need to connect with others to assure themselves they're okay, *normal*; affixing themselves to someone similar and therefore easy to manipulate. Just find their itch, then, scratch it — simple.

After all, all of us are islands, separate, egocentric whether we like it or not. However, they're equipped with draw-bridges able to be lowered or closed. But the thing about drawbridges is that they offer their owner choices. Is this person enemy or foe? Should I lower my bridge? Allow them entry? And this choice, together with their need to connect, is their weakness — their itch.

Whereas to continue the analogy, it's not that I don't have a drawbridge because I do. Mary, Julie, and Janice, for example, were allowed entry — but for an entirely different purpose. And it's not that I don't have a need to connect; it's that I can't. Therefore, if I'm offering entry, naturally it must be to my advantage. I mean, it's only human, isn't it? *That's funny, Jocelyn.* I quite often amuse myself with such witticisms. Amuse, but never to the point of laughter or even a chuckle. Perhaps a smirk. There you go again — so droll.

As for my daughter, apart from her continual suppression as she was growing up, I wasn't exactly sure what big plans I had in store for her until Gordon came into my life as a patient; his repressed memory and his kinky, sexual response stirred my intrigue no end. What if Janice were to react the same way? Like Gordon, she too had repressed the memory of her own, nearly identical experience. And, as Rob was secretly my patient after a friendly lunch with him when, as easily as opening a sardine can, he'd opened up to me, I knew how loveless their marriage was. So Officer Manning and I, with Rob's unwitting assistance, set everything in train, she seducing the poor bastard before coming up with *their* particular *plan* — if you could call an affair such.

And now, surprisingly, it's all turned out honky-dory for everyone. Not that that worries me. My protagonist's unhappiness or happiness is of no real concern. As long as I'm the one pulling the strings, then que sera, sera, whatever will be will be. Like a novelist allowing their protagonists to find their own path with the character he or she has created for them.

Sitting back, sipping on my black sugarless tea, I savour its taste, looking forward to my latest project involving my recent, susceptible patient while also following with interest my daughter's continued developments, wondering where in blazes they'll lead her. Her life, as it has been ever since her *incident* — a continued source of fascination for me.

Janice

With the nasty business of controlling Officer Manning behind us, Gordon and I drive back to his country residence — the sorting out of our own lives next on my list.

"So, in the words of a famous song, *what now, my love?*" I ask.

"Well, as Officer Manning explained, we still have to complete the program so she can show the time-stamped photos to the magistrate to sign off on her dropping your charge."

"I know that, Gordon," I say. "You're obfuscating, confusing things as per usual."

"In what way?"

"I'm talking about *us*," I say. "How are we going to play things?"

"*Play* things?"

"Stop it. I know all these tricks people play," I say." I've made a study of them plying my trade."

"Like your mother."

I glance across, giving him a look as much to say *be careful.* He may well be my master, have me *collared,* as they say. But outside of the bedroom, he's an absolute pussy cat, one of the many things I so admire about him. What was it that Abraham Lincoln said, and I paraphrase. *If you want to find the true test of a man's character, don't give him adversity. Give him power.* And my beautiful man is the precise example of this. The tighter he ties me, the more considerate he becomes, which jells perfectly with my mindset. I'm not here to be humiliated or told what *a useless bit of shit I am*. No, I'm here to be glorified by the caress of his bonds.

I've only been under his guardianship for twenty-seven days, but in that short time, I've learnt so much about myself; this practical experience is an addition to the research I'd undertaken upon learning of my fate. There's no way an analytical being like me would enter into such a vulnerable commitment without proper research, for as Mother had often told me, *knowledge is power Janice, so study hard.* And charged with the energy of enthusiasm, I did, reading everything I could about BDSM. But I soon found that there was a lot more to it than any amount of book reading could show me.

People think that bondage is of the one stripe. But like every other subject on earth, it's not. It has as many variations as lovemaking itself. And I don't mean that in the Kama Sutra, positional sense, but more the psychological context surrounding it. For instance, the term BDSM, bondage, discipline, sadism, masochism. Most people who are into bondage are not into pain. To those who seek the solace that masochism can bring, bondage is merely a means to an end. In fact, a great deal of them merely *assume the position* — male and female alike — by slipping their hands into silk loopholes positioned for such purpose before allowing themselves to be flogged mercilessly. It's not a matter of power to them but more about receiving the gift of pain from their loved one.

Gordon and I are not like that. But even so, our shenanigans are nuanced. I'm so into power — losing it, that is — but only when under the care of my loved one, as shown by my negative reaction when left alone at the police station. However, my beautiful man is not. To him, his rigging is a work of art, technical expertise, engineering, all done with the sole purpose of objectifying me into an intricate, imaginative sculpture—an object of beauty.

And I'm so into his work, specifically when it's carried out on me and when I become the centre of his devoted, extreme attention. Fuck me, how many people are loved like that? Such that our mutual desire for my utter captivity allows us both to explore our individual obsessions. That's what I've found bondage facilitates, making it easy to achieve our objectives of having our minds blown away. His by his absolute artistry, his crafting of me into the *perfect imagery of womanhood, femininity* or whatever it is in that weird, wonderful mind of his, and mine by my complete and utter captivity under the care of one whose love and consideration I can sense with every tug of his loving ropes. Or, as in the case of our aforementioned masochistic cousins—with every stroke of their lover's whip.

Oh, what a magical web we weave, when pure love we do conceive. Maybe Shakespeare or Sir Walter Scott, or whoever the fuck supposedly wrote the original, was into bondage? *LOL.*

With my mind returning to the present, I turn into Gordon's estate and enter his code and then wait for the gate to slowly open while staring at him.

"What?" he says.

"I'm just wondering what our life will be like without our artificial conditions."

"Artificial?"

"Yes," I say. My structured, institutionalised captivity has an utter helplessness—an inevitability about it. I had no choice in the matter . . . something our future consensual relationship can never hope to achieve."

"And you don't think that could be created again?"

I'm startled by this. "How could it be?" I ask. "I have no

intention of ever littering again or doing anything that could in the slightest be considered criminal."

"Fantasy, darling, fantasy," he says.

I drive through the open gates, stop the car, and then turn off the engine before looking him square in the eye. "Explain yourself."

"Well, first of all, consensually submitting to your lover has its own appeal, darling. Remember, I've been married before, and the thrill of having a partner who's prepared to submit herself willingly is as exciting an experience as one could ever ask for. Heavens, that's true commitment."

Jesus, I'm experiencing a warm tingle below.

"Exactly," he says.

God, he knows me too well.

"And as for your future enforced captivity. This property is always available to relive this amazing time."

"But it must be structured," I say. "We'll have to set a time, perhaps every three months, where we'll take a week off, and you transport me in the van as once you did, my love."

Fuck me, my pussy is salivating.

"But giving you your instructions as you stand there at ease beforehand."

Starting the car, I look straight ahead as I drive up his long driveway, my need for his special love as urgent as it's ever been.

EPILOGUE

Jocelyn

Sitting on the bench in my garden in the warm summer night — my favourite place in the world — not for the first time in the last few days, I reflect on where life has taken me. Or, to be more accurate, where I have taken it and everyone around me.

I say *my favourite place*. But not for nostalgic, romantic reasons as most would. No, what makes anything favourite in my life is something that reminds me of past successes. This particular instance, on my bench under the maple tree, reminding me of my most important triumph — for beneath my feet lie the remains of my dearly departed husband.

It was not I that came upon his evil that night. Indeed, the opposite. I was the one fascinated by the Armchair Thriller episodes — not him. Wondering what it would be like for someone to actually be imprisoned like that, I'd decided to try it out on my daughter. Why not? She was mine, plus she deserved it. Unfortunately, her father had unexpectedly come home early that night, just after I'd locked Janice away — the very beginning of my torment and oppression of her life.

Having crossed a certain line that night where fantasies had turned into actions, I decided to kill two birds with one stone, so to speak. Luring him out to the garden with a couple of glasses of red, I'd smashed him across the back of his head with the side of a garden spade, damn near decapitating him.

The soil in our yard is quite arable. Even so, it took me

about an hour to dig the six-foot hole that I rolled his lifeless body into. I had then refilled it before planting the now large maple tree above it, giving myself an alibi if anyone ever asked about the disturbance of the soil. Of course no one ever did. Barbecues with friends were hardly the events our family engaged in. Indeed, Janice was the only other soul that ventured out there, though very rarely, due to my continual banishing of her to her room.

That was why she was left in the cupboard for such a long while as I, with a cap on my head, large, dark glasses and his overcoat on, took her father's car to the airport and left it there before returning via public transport. It was longer than I had planned for her to be locked away, four hours in all, with her body reacting alarmingly when I first touched it to untie her. Any wonder she repressed her memory, a fortunate circumstance as it turned out.

I'll leave Janice and Gordon alone for now. I have my new patient. Allow my darling daughter to immerse herself in her new-found libido, maybe even present me with a grandchild or two. That will be a new experience, one worth waiting for, and as I'm back in her good books, I'll have loads of access to them. Perhaps even being asked to babysit them, creating a couple of new masterpieces.

Sipping on my wine, with my husband lying below, I feel . . . happy? Is that what this is? I'll have to explore that further with my new subject and discover what similar emotions I can ignite from the embers of her deeply depressed soul. Perhaps even use Gordon's psychological program to bring the best out of her. Jesus, imagine that? An already tortured soul being exposed to his methods. Of course I won't tell him of her true symptoms, suggest another malady more suited to his deranged methods. Perhaps even get her on a diversion program. Hmm, now there's a thought. She did confess some minor arson to me. Officer Manning would be interested in that. Who knows where such an environment could take my vulnerable patient? Who knows? Who knows?

The End

About the Author

Stephen Mottram is a retired grandfather of three who lives in Melbourne Australia. After retiring Stephen re-educated himself, studying various subjects at a tertiary level including philosophy, astronomy, fine drawing and history. However he draws most of his knowledge from his own very interesting life, a life where he explored his own humanity to the fullest, garnering many wonderful experiences and meeting some amazing people along the way. Stephen uses these life experiences in his writing, injecting a whimsical and informative style to all of his books and gifting his readers with an individual and interesting perspective on humanity where he exposes both its wonderful frailties and its astonishing strengths.

www.ingramcontent.com/pod-product-compliance
Lightning Source LLC
Chambersburg PA
CBHW071715140626
46557CB00011B/499